LIVE THIS LOVE

JAMEY MOODY

CONTENTS

Connect   v
Also by Jamey Moody   vii

Chapter 1   1
Chapter 2   17
Chapter 3   34
Chapter 4   53
Chapter 5   69
Chapter 6   84
Chapter 7   98
Chapter 8   115
Chapter 9   126
Chapter 10   142
Chapter 11   156
Chapter 12   169
Chapter 13   176
Chapter 14   190

About the Author   195
Also by Jamey Moody   197

Live This Love

© 2020 by Jamey Moody. All Rights Reserved.

Edited: Jessica Hatch

Proofread: Monna Herring

Cover: Magnolia Robbins

This is a work of fiction. Names, characters, places, and incidents are the product of the author's imagination or are used fictitiously. Any resemblance to an actual person, living or dead, business establishments, events, or locales is entirely coincidental.

This book, or parts thereof, may not be reproduced in any form without permission.

❀ Created with Vellum

CONNECT

Thank you for purchasing my book! I hope you enjoy the story.

If you'd like to stay updated on future releases, you can visit my website or sign up for my mailing list here.
www.jameymoodyauthor.com

As an independent author, reviews are greatly appreciated.

I'd love to hear from you!
email: jameymoodyauthor@gmail.com

ALSO BY JAMEY MOODY

The Your Way Series

Finding Home

Finding Family

Finding Forever

It Takes A Miracle

One Little Yes

The Lovers Landing Series

Where Secrets Are Safe

No More Secrets

And The Truth Is ...

1

Something was coming. Something that gives an eerie feeling, that makes the hair stand up on the back of your neck, that gives you butterflies in your stomach, a tingling in your arms and legs. That's what Alex Adams knew the minute she woke up that morning in June: something was coming and it was coming for her.

She knew something was coming just as sure as she knew there would be a beautiful sunset this evening. The sunset was beautiful nearly every evening on St. John. The sunsets, the beaches, and the laidback island vibe brought tourists to this remote part of the United States year round.

The weather forecast was for sunny skies and a light breeze, so Peaches would be hopping that night. Peaches was the bar that Alex co-owned and one of the best spots for locals and tourists to watch the sunset. It was an open-air bar with a patio and small area for a band and dancing. It was on the main street of town, but the beach was just out the back door and across the patio. It was rustic but brightly painted and welcoming. Alex lived in a small apartment above the bar, so she was always nearby if her employees needed help. Alex loved the bar, the locals, the tourists, and especially Liz Medina, her co-owner.

"What are you doing here before noon? I thought you were helping me this evening so Beverly could leave early," Alex said as Liz walked into the bar.

"Oh, I am. I was out and about and thought I'd take my favorite manager to lunch. What do you say? Fish tacos with pineapple salsa are calling my name," Liz said as she smacked her lips.

At sixty-four years old Liz had seen the ebb and flow of island life and how people fall in love with it. Too many times Liz had seen people move to the islands to get away from something or start over just to learn they weren't cut out for the full-time island life. Alex had walked into Liz's bar one sunny afternoon sixteen years ago and felt an immediate connection. It had been the first time in a long time she felt like she could breathe.

Everyone was welcome in Peaches, but Liz had a reputation for loving the ladies, so the crowd was often filled with lesbians. In fact, it wasn't unusual for Alex to be invited back to someone's hotel. Sometimes she accepted, but she never took anyone home with her. Above the bar was her safe haven, and she refused to share it with anyone.

"Well, I had a late breakfast this morning because I was out riding my bike and let time get away from me," said Alex. She usually biked, ran, or paddle-boarded every morning. Exercise had always been her drug of choice, and it relaxed her. It also gave her a toned, tanned body that belied her forty-six years. She looked ten years younger, with sun-lightened brown hair whose streaks of gold stopped at her shoulders. Her brown eyes were the color of a fine whiskey and held a secret no one knew but Liz.

"Hmm, now what were you thinking on to make you

lose track of time, Miss-I'm-Never-Late-for-Anything-and-Stick-to-My-Schedule?"

Alex didn't say anything.

Liz raised her eyebrows, creasing her forehead, and said, "Come on, out with it. What's going on, Alex?"

"Oh nothing."

"Really? You expect me to believe nothing is going on when I could set my watch by your morning routine. What's up?" Liz demanded.

"I don't know, Liz. I have this feeling something is coming. I can't explain it, just a feeling," Alex confessed.

"Well, let's see. The best I remember, when you have one of these feelings"—she used her hands to form air quotes around the word—"good things usually happen. Like the time Hurricane Irma was supposed to miss the island and you had us prepare and take shelter anyway. You saved a lot of people that day if you'll remember. So don't let it bother you."

"I'm not letting it bother me. It's just kind of nagging at me, you know," said Alex.

"Look, kiddo, that's one reason I wanted us to have lunch. Your whole world is this bar, and that nagging feeling you've got is going to be me if you don't stop and look at where you're living!"

"Huh? What do you mean where I'm living? I know where I am, and I happen to love my job," Alex said with a perplexed look on her face.

"I know you do. But honey, you're living in a paradise most people only dream about. Take some time and enjoy it," Liz said. "You open up most days and are here to close every night. You rarely take a night off. You should ask one of the beautiful girls that come in here looking for an island fling to go out. And I don't mean to this bar!"

"Come on, Liz. Not this again. You know these girls are here for a few days and gone," replied Alex.

"I'm not saying fall in love. I'm saying have a little fun, share a meal, do a little dancing, walk on the beach, and have hot sex!" Liz said as she twirled in a circle and did a hip thrust.

Alex's jaw fell open and eyes went wide. "Oh my god, you just can't stop yourself sometimes, can you?"

"I'm serious. I see how these girls look at you. Hell, they used to look at me the same way. And I don't mind telling you I had some good times along the way especially when I was your age."

"I know. And it wasn't that long ago I saw you leave with one of those 'girls,'" said Alex.

"This isn't about me. All I'm saying is don't sell yourself short. Just because you see me alone and occasionally leaving with someone doesn't mean that's how it will be for you too." Liz took a breath. "I don't want to see you pass something or someone up because you are chained to this bar. You can have both and be happy."

"Okay. But do you mind telling me where all this is coming from?" Alex asked.

"Honestly, I came across this picture and it got me thinking," Liz admitted as she showed the photo to Alex.

In the photograph, they were on the bar patio. Liz was sitting at a table with her arm around a beautiful woman. Alex stood behind the two with her arms around both of them. Strings of lights twinkled overhead and reflected in their eyes as their smiles brightened the night.

"You were just a baby. I think you'd just gotten here," Liz said.

"Yeah, I remember this. I'd been here about a month.

That's the lovely Lorna. She tried so hard to get you to leave with her. I recall tears when she left."

"Yep. Tears from us both." Liz sighed.

"I often wondered if she'd have come here a year later if you would have gone with her. By then you knew I was staying and would take care of the bar for you, so you could have at least given it a chance," Alex said quietly.

"Maybe. I thought about contacting her from time to time over the years but didn't," Liz said with a wistful look on her face. She shook her head. "But this picture made me think that I don't want you to miss a similar opportunity. As I look back now I do wonder, 'What if?' I don't want you to look back in ten or twenty years and wonder 'what if', Alex."

Alex's eyebrows raised, but she didn't say anything.

"All I'm asking is for you to keep an open mind and remember where you are. Love is all around this paradise because that's what people come here for. It wouldn't hurt you to grab a little for yourself," Liz explained.

"Okay. I see what you're saying. But you know a long-term love isn't in the cards for me. There's no way anyone would want to be with me if they knew the reason I stayed here. And I don't know how I'd even try to tell someone. They'd run before I finished the story."

"Don't be so sure, Alex. People will surprise you, especially if the right one just so happens to walk into our bar. I know you don't believe that right now, but keep an open mind. And take a walk on the beach with a beautiful woman for goodness sake! Okay?" Liz demanded.

"Okay, Liz. Can we talk about this liquor order now?" Alex asked, successfully putting an end to the discussion.

Alex was right: tables were filling up at Peaches as the sun went down. It'd be a busy night. She didn't mind, though; she loved to watch the people. They came from all over, ready to play on the beach, walk along and stop in the little shops, and enjoy their time at the bar.

Liz and Alex were tending bar while Max and Danny waited tables. It wouldn't be long until Max's shift ended; then the remaining three would handle the rest of the night. They had all worked together for a few years and were a smoothly running team. On weekend nights the bar could get crowded, and it looked like this Friday night wouldn't be any different. They kept everyone happy, with the drinks flowing and music playing. Occasionally there would be the impatient tourist that had too much to drink and wanted more, but it wasn't anything they couldn't handle.

When a group of eight women walked in, the bar's volume rose noticeably. Danny leaned against the bar and said, "I think it's a birthday party." Then he greeted the group and showed them to a table.

"Sorority sisters," Max guessed.

"Old college friends having a reunion," Liz added.

Alex shook her head. "Nah, that's a wedding party."

When Danny brought their drink order back to the bar, he laughed and said, "Surprise, surprise, it's a lesbian wedding. That's the third one this week."

"I win," Alex said. "Pay up."

"Who said anything about betting this time?" complained Max.

"We're always betting, you know that," said Liz. "We'll take it out of the tips tonight."

"Works for me. Now let's get these ladies their drinks. First round is on the house, best wishes to the brides!" Alex said as she and Liz started filling glasses with ice.

* * *

As their server led them to the table, Riley James made sure she wasn't sitting by Lee. Since they landed on St. John this morning Lee had made it obvious she was interested in a wedding party hook-up with Riley, but that wasn't happening. Lee was a friend of a friend and had tried this before with Riley at the last party they both attended. She remembered Lee left with someone else after Riley repeatedly dodged her. Lee thought she was God's gift to women but Riley wanted nothing to do with her. All Riley wanted to do was celebrate her friends Kim and Kerry's wedding. After fifteen years together they'd finally decided to tie the knot.

She managed to sit next to Kim, while Kara, Riley's best friend, was on her other side. Next to Kara were Julie and Sara, who had been married for ten years. Lee sat next to them, and Lisa, Kerry's sister, rounded out the group. The eight friends all knew Kim and Kerry well but couldn't necessarily say the same about each other. Still, it was a good group with varied backgrounds that all loved the brides-to-be.

Riley was looking forward to the next two weeks since she and Kara had decided to turn this into a vacation. Her plan was the wedding and then sun and fun. She was open to anything at this point. As of last week she was now a retired teacher and not sure what comes next. Maybe she would island hop all summer or have a torrid summer fling with a younger woman.

When the waiter brought the first round of drinks, he declared that it was on the house. That got a cheer from the group. Kerry immediately ordered a round of shots for everyone and gave a toast. "I know it's taken us too long to finally tie the knot, but we're certainly not too old to party, so let's pretend we're still dirty, thirty, and silly!"

The group laughed and cheered as the party started.

"Come on, let's dance!" Kerry got up and led Kim to the dance floor.

"Sorry, Lee, I haven't had near enough to drink to dance. Thanks, though," Riley replied with a shake of her curly dark red hair.

"Come on, Lee, I'll dance with you," Lisa said. She grabbed Lee's hand and headed to the dance floor.

"I think Lee is definitely interested in you being her wedding fling," Kara observed.

"Well, she needs to get uninterested real quick because that ain't happening. No way," Riley said emphatically.

"I'd help you out with Lee, but she's not really my type. Besides she couldn't keep up with me," Kara said as she looked around the bar.

"I don't even want to know what you mean by that," Riley said.

Kara chuckled as she nudged Riley with her shoulder. "Now there's someone more your type. Check out the bartender. Maybe she'd show us around since we're staying after the wedding."

Riley followed Kara's gaze. A sexy, toned bartender with light brown hair pulled into a messy pony tail was lining up the glasses for their shots. "Are you kidding me? I'm sure she could have her pick any night."

"She could show us around, tell us the good places to go, take you for a long walk on the beach," Kara said, wiggling her eyebrows up and down.

"Oh my god." Riley rolled her eyes.

Kara pulled her face into a pout. "Come on, Riley, you haven't dated anyone in forever. How long has it been since you had—wait, don't answer that. Besides, I've seen her looking over here checking you out. You should go talk to her."

"How do you know she was checking me out? There were eight people sitting here. Besides, what makes you think she bats for our team?" Riley said.

"We're about to find out," Kara said as Danny walked back to their table with the shots. "Hey, Danny, right?"

"Yeah, that's right," Danny said as he set the drinks on the table.

"I have a question for you. We were just wondering if the bartender was 'Family', you know what I mean?" Kara asked, raising her eyebrows.

Danny laughed. "Yeah, I hear you, and yes, Alex is into women."

"Alex, huh? Does she have a girlfriend, Danny?" Kara continued.

"Nope."

"Leave Danny alone, Kara. That's enough questions," Riley interrupted, saving Danny and herself from further embarrassment.

"Let me know if you need anything else," Danny said, smiling as he walked away.

As the evening continued so did the drinking and the dancing. Alex kept a watchful eye over the bar. It was her job to make sure everyone had a good time but was also respectful of others. There were several tables now interacting with one another, and it looked like a huge party. Everyone was having a good time, especially the brides and their group. Alex loved to see women having a good time and wondered to herself how old they were, where they came from, and what they did for a living. It was a game she played nearly every night, though tonight she couldn't seem to keep her eyes off the woman with short red hair. There was something about her.

Alex had made eye contact with her a couple of times

when she took drinks to the table. The woman had blue-green eyes and a really nice smile. At least, it certainly was nice when she smiled at Alex. It didn't appear like she was with anyone in particular. She had danced with one of the other women from her table, but looked to be actively trying to avoid another. Alex didn't really have time to think about it, though, because she was busy tending the bar. The next thing she knew, she looked up and there the redhead was at the end of her bar.

"Can I get you something?" Alex said.

"Could you make me a glass of water and make it look like a drink?" the redhead asked. "I don't want my friends teasing me about not keeping up."

Alex chuckled. "Sure, we'll fix up sparkling water with a little lemon, a sword with pineapple and cherry, and a tiny umbrella." She fiddled around behind the bar before plopping a rocks glass in front of the woman. "How's that?"

"Perfect. The umbrella is a nice touch," she said as she took a sip. "My friends want to party like when we were young and dumb, but someone has to hold it together to get us back to the hotel eventually."

Alex smiled. Looking out for others, that's nice.

"Something funny?" the woman asked.

"No, not at all. It just looks like you may have lost a couple of your friends," Alex said as she nodded at the exit toward the beach. One of the woman's friends was laughing and strolling away with a stranger, and another from the group was nowhere to be found.

"Well, let's hope they're just going for a little walk on the beach." And then she saw the woman she'd been avoiding looking around for her. She quickly turned back to the bar and groaned, "Please take a hint and hit on someone else."

"Excuse me—" Alex exclaimed.

"No, no. I didn't mean you! I'm sorry, one of our friends keeps hitting on me and won't take a hint," the woman explained.

"I kind of noticed you were trying to avoid her earlier and wondered if there was a problem."

"No, there's not a problem," she sighed. "I don't really know her that well and don't want to, I might add, but she is persistent. That's why I came up here to get a drink and get away for a bit."

Liz had been listening to their conversation and chose that moment to walk around the bar and pat the woman's shoulder. "Let me see what I can do about that." She intercepted her friend, put her arm around her, and led her back to the patio.

"What's she telling her?" the woman asked Alex.

Alex shook her head and laughed. "There's not much telling, but probably something like, 'Let me show you what other karaoke songs we have.' Liz has a way with women, you might say."

"Well, thank you, Liz! By the way, thanks for that first round of drinks. We all appreciated it. And I'm Riley," she said sticking out her hand to Alex.

"No problem, but how do you know I'm the one that did that?" Alex asked, taking Riley's hand.

"Our waiter told me."

"I'm Alex. Nice to meet you, Riley," she said holding Riley's hand and looking into her eyes. "A wedding is always a reason to celebrate, and Peaches just wanted to be part of it."

"Well, thank you," Riley said. She didn't really want to let Alex's hand go. It felt so warm and strong and her hand fit like it belonged there.

"When is the ceremony? I hope it's not tomorrow

because I don't care how young y'all are—I don't think the brides will be feeling so perky in the morning." Alex nodded her head to the dance floor.

Riley turned and saw her friends in a conga line flowing around the dance floor. "Oh wow," she commented. "There will be some hangovers in their future, but just look how much fun they're having!"

Riley watched Alex fill several orders and smile her way occasionally. It was a bit mesmerizing how smooth she was, how at ease with each customer. Riley liked the smiles Alex sent her way. She realized that while she'd been talking and watching Alex it had been a while since she'd seen Kara or Lisa.

"As much as I've been enjoying talking to you, especially without Lee hanging around, I think I'd better go check on Kara and Lisa," she said. "It won't be long before we have to catch the ferry back to our hotel." When she looked at the bartender, they held one another's eyes a little longer than necessary. "It was really nice to meet you, Alex. You mix a mean sparkling water. I hope to see you again."

"It was nice to meet you too, Riley. I hope you find your friends and have a great time in the islands. Come back any time," Alex said with a big smile on her face that she wasn't sure why was it there. She almost offered to help find her friends, but the bar was still pretty busy.

* * *

Riley had been up and down the beach several times. The first time she saw Lisa right away and reminded her that they had to catch a ferry back to their hotel on St. Thomas. Lisa told her she'd meet them at the dock. She had actually run into an old friend from college, and they were catching up. She assured Riley she wouldn't miss the boat.

As Riley stopped in a few bars along the beach looking for Kara, she couldn't stop thinking about Alex. She'd heard all the stories about having a fling while on vacation and had never thought it could happen to her until she started talking to the bartender. Alex was more than a bartender, she'd learned from Danny. Not only did she work there but she owned the bar with Liz, was single, and was an "awesome person," as Danny put it.

Before leaving she'd have to be sure and thank Liz for getting rid of Lee for her. At least she had a little peace to enjoy her fake drink with Alex. Hmm, with Alex. It wasn't like she was having a drink with her. It was Alex's job to mix drinks, pour beer, and be friendly, right? After all she did run a bar, and keeping people there to buy drinks was her business. If she was friendly, folks would stay there longer. Even so, Riley thought she had felt something every time Alex smiled her way. Surely she was imagining it.

Come on, you'll be fifty years old in a few months, she thought to herself. *Alex is beautiful and owns a bar on an island in paradise for goodness' sake, she could have her pick any night. She was just being friendly, she's not interested in you.*

Time was getting away from her as she mused about Alex. She still hadn't found Kara. She'd texted her several times, but no reply. When her phone finally pinged, she was relieved to see her best friend's name on the screen.

Kara: Hey, I saw Lisa and she said you were looking for me. I'll meet you at the bar.

All good, wink, wink.

Riley: Of course it is. Ok. Haha.

. . .

As she headed back to Peaches, she thought they might be cutting it a little close to catch their ferry, but surely there would be others.

* * *

Alex cleared off the empty tables as folks headed to the dock to catch the last ferry of the day. A few people remained that were staying on St. John. It had been a good evening and night. The bar never was too crowded, but it was full and everyone seemed to have a good time.

After Riley left, Alex would find her mind drifting back to the redhead and her amazing eyes. She could feel Riley watching her as she filled orders and helped customers. She couldn't help looking over at her and smiling. Alex thought she could get lost in those eyes and they'd never let her go. Maybe she wouldn't want them to.

"What are you thinking?" Alex chided herself. She could tell Riley wasn't the kind of woman for a vacation fling. Even if she was, she was busy with her friends. And what would she want with a bartender?

"Hey, Alex," Danny yelled. "These ladies need to talk to you."

Alex went over to the table where she found Riley's friends. "Do you know where Riley went? I saw her talking to you earlier," the one she thought Riley had called Kim slurred.

"She went to look for a couple of your party that had left," Alex told her.

"Okay. We were heading back to catch the ferry and didn't want to leave her. If she comes back here, will you tell her we all went back to the hotel, please?" Kim said while swaying a little.

"Are you sure you can make it? I'd be happy to send someone to the dock with you," Alex said.

"We're okay," Kerry said. "Yes, we've all had a little too much to drink but not so much that we can't walk," she added with a smile. "Thanks for such a fun night. You've got a great place here. Hopefully we'll be back before we head home."

"Congrats to y'all, by the way, on the wedding," Alex said. "Thanks for coming to Peaches. We loved having your whole group."

They waved goodbye and made their way out of the bar and up the street. Alex looked at her watch and hoped Riley would come back by.

She was busy cleaning up tables, tidying up what she could and checking the receipts and inventory. She guessed that Riley had met her friends back at the dock. She admitted to herself that she was a little disappointed.

"What's the sad look for?" Liz asked.

"What sad look?"

"The one on your face. I was watching how deep in thought you were, and then your face fell. It wouldn't have to do with that pretty little redhead I saved earlier, would it?" Liz said with raised eyebrows. "You know, the one that was chatting you up at the bar and couldn't keep her eyes off you."

Alex just looked at Liz.

"That's why I so kindly distracted her friend," Liz said, as though this were the most obvious thing in the world. "I saw how she looked at you, and I hoped you'd go for it after our discussion earlier."

"She had to go find her other friend. I guess she found her and caught the ferry because her friends left a while ago. She must not have been as interested as you thought," Alex said quietly.

"So that *is* the reason for the long face," Liz said.

"Okay, I'll admit I was hoping she'd come back by, but I guess I missed my chance," Alex said.

Liz's sympathetic look transformed into a look of excitement so quickly that Alex had to wonder if she was feeling okay.

"Well, here's your second chance." Liz nodded toward the back of the bar. "Your mysterious redhead just walked through the patio door. Don't mess this one up, honey," she said, and busied herself with the cash drawer.

2

Riley walked into the bar and looked around for her friends, but they were nowhere to be found. That was odd, she thought. Weren't they all going to walk to the dock to catch the ferry?

She noticed the bartender, Alex, at the bar, so Riley walked over. "Hey, I don't guess you'd know where my friends are? I thought we were leaving here together to catch the ferry."

Alex looked up and seemed excited to see her. "Oh, hey. They left some time ago and asked me to tell you they'd meet you at the hotel."

"At the hotel? I thought we were walking to the dock together."

"I thought you must've met them at the dock. I'm sure they caught the last ferry," Alex said.

Riley's eyes grew wide. "Last ferry? You mean the ferry doesn't run all the time?"

"No, the last one left about a half hour ago."

Her heart dropped into her stomach. "So, if there's no

other ferry how do I get back to the hotel? Is there another way?"

"Uh, not really, Riley. Most of the water taxis don't run at night."

"Seriously? I'm stuck here until morning?" Riley looked around wondering what she should do next. Would she have to sleep on the street? "You're kidding. Do you all live on this island? There's not some boat I could catch?"

"I'm really sorry, but everyone I know has already left for the night," Alex said.

Riley stood there for a moment thinking. "Well, I guess I'd better go find me a hotel for the night. Damn, I can't believe this! I'm the one that tries to make sure everyone gets where we need to be, and I miss the last ferry!" She threw her arms up in the air. "Perfect."

Later, Alex couldn't be sure what made her do it. Maybe it was the woman's air of hopelessness or her own do-gooder heart. "I tell you what, Riley," she said. "Have a seat and I'll pour you a beer. Check in with your friends and see where they are. I'll call around and see if I can get you a place to stay tonight. How's that sound?"

Riley looked at Alex as she poured the beer and sighed. "That would be really nice. Thanks, Alex."

"No problem. I'll be right back." Alex went to the end of the bar and got her phone while Riley texted Kara.

Riley: Hey, where are you? I'm at the bar and you're not here.

Kara: You're here? I've been waiting on you for an hour! I don't see you.

Riley: What? I'm sitting at the bar.

Kara: You're not at the bar because that's where I am.

Riley: I'm at Peaches, sitting at the bar!

Kara: Peaches!? I'm at the hotel bar!

Riley: The hotel bar? Why are you at the hotel bar?

Kara: You said you would meet me at the bar. I've been here for an hour waiting on you!

Riley: Shit! I thought you meant to meet at Peaches and we'd take the ferry back with everyone else.

Kara: Everyone is here!

Riley: Great! I'm stuck here because the last ferry left 30 minutes ago while I was waiting on you to get back from your little walk on the beach!

Kara: Holy shit, Riley!! I'm so sorry! What are you going to do?

Riley: Alex is calling a couple of places to see if I can get a room for the night. I can't fucking believe this!

Kara: Alex? Bartender Alex?

Riley: Yes.

Kara: This might not be so bad after all! ;) Let me know where you end up.

Riley: Not even funny! I'll see you in the morning when I can catch a boat.

Breathe, Riley, she said to herself. That's why you've been learning to meditate. She took several deep breaths and let them out slowly with her eyes closed.

"Are you all right?" Alex asked.

Riley's eyes popped open to see Alex standing in front of her. "Yeah, I was just trying to calm down."

"Did it work?"

She pushed out a breath, shakier than the last few. "Not sure yet. It turns out Kara, the one that's supposed to be my best friend, is waiting for me at the hotel bar." She picked up her glass and gave the beer a sour look. "I thought she meant this bar obviously."

"Maybe you should take a few more of those deep breaths," said Alex.

"No, I'm fine," Riley said, but Alex had begun to look

uncomfortable. "Wait, why do you say that?"

"Well, I'm afraid the places I'd recommend for you to stay tonight are full," Alex said apologetically as Riley's face fell and her shoulders sagged defeated. "But I have an idea," she quickly added. Riley looked up.

"I happen to live above the bar and have a very comfortable couch. You're welcome to stay with me," Alex said.

"Oh, I couldn't put you out like that." Or could I, Riley thought, she's beautiful and willing to rescue me.

"You wouldn't be putting me out. I wouldn't offer if I didn't want you to," Alex said.

Riley narrowed her eyes. "Really?"

Alex nodded.

"You're not the island serial killer or anything like that, right?"

"No, they caught him last month. You're safe here," Alex said with a laugh.

"Well, if you're sure they caught him, I gratefully accept your kindness."

"Great. I have a few things to finish up here, but I can take you up and show you around first if you want," Alex said.

"Show you around where?" Liz walked up to the pair.

"It seems that my friends and I had a major miscommunication," Riley explained. "They left me and I missed the last ferry. Alex has graciously offered to let me spend the night and catch the boat in the morning."

"Oh she did, did she?" Liz said with raised eyebrows.

Riley noticed Alex give Liz a weird look, but she forged ahead anyway. "She did, and I couldn't be more grateful. I promise to bring my friends back and make them spend lots of money in here to make up for it. By the way, thanks for the distraction earlier with Lee."

Liz chuckled. "You're most welcome. Danny and I have this. You two go ahead, and we'll close up."

"You don't have to," Alex protested. "It won't take me long to finish up."

"I know it won't, but I've got this. Get Riley settled in. See you both tomorrow," Liz said and started cleaning up.

"Right this way." Alex led her guest to a door at the end of the bar. "You might want to take my hand, it's a little dark in here and I don't want you to miss a step."

Riley took Alex's hand and once again noticed how their hands fit perfectly together as she followed her through the door and up a flight of stairs. She couldn't help but be a little excited. While walking on the beach earlier her mind had wandered to thoughts of Alex, and what she was like. It looked like she was going to get the chance to learn more, and that suited her just fine.

"Come on in," Alex said. She unlocked the door and moved aside so Riley could enter.

Riley found herself in one large room. On the left was a living area with a couch, TV, a couple of chairs, and a table. Directly ahead was the kitchen area, and off to her right were two open doors. There were windows everywhere, making the room look larger than it was. Alex definitely had a beach vibe going, with muted tones of blue, green, and tan. The floors were hardwood with throw rugs of the same colors. It was welcoming, comfy, and homey.

"What a great place. It's beautiful—and all those windows!" Riley said.

"Thanks. On your left you'll notice the living area and across is the kitchen. This door is to the bathroom, and this one is to the bedroom," Alex said pointing to each door. "It's not much, but really it's perfect for me."

"I love it. Who needs a bunch of rooms?" Riley said, then chided herself for making such a dumb comment.

"Would you like to see the rest? I mean there's another great view I'd like you to see," Alex said as she walked to the bedroom door.

"I would," Riley said following Alex into the bedroom. One entire wall was windows with a door that opened to a small deck that faced the ocean. For a moment she wondered what it would be like waking up with Alex in this room.

She shook the thought out of her head and said, "What a beautiful view! I'm sure it never gets old waking up to this every morning."

Alex smiled and said, "Let me show you my favorite spot." She opened the door to the deck and walked to her right. Riley followed her as she turned up another small flight of stairs that led to the roof. As Riley walked onto the roof she was bowled over by all the stars shining overhead. There was a low couch with end tables on each side and a small table with two chairs that looked out over the ocean. It took her breath away.

After a few moments Riley said in a hushed voice, "My god, Alex, this is beautiful."

"It really is. For me, this is paradise. I don't care what kind of day I've had. Everything is erased when I come up here," Alex said softly.

"I can understand that," Riley said, still gazing over the water and at the stars above.

"Are you hungry?"

Riley realized she hadn't eaten anything since a late lunch that day, and immediately her stomach growled. "I didn't realize until you asked, but yeah, I am," she admitted.

"Let's go downstairs and I'll make you something," Alex said.

"Oh, I don't want to be any more trouble."

"It's no trouble. I was going to make me something anyway."

"Would you mind if we stayed up here a little longer? It's all so gorgeous," Riley said looking into Alex's eyes and holding them there. She thought those might be the warmest brown eyes she'd ever looked into.

Alex realized she was staring, cleared her throat and said, "Sure, let me get you something to drink. I have a small refrigerator up here." She made her way to one of the tables at the end of the couch and opened the mini fridge. "I have beer or water. I'm the only one that comes up here, so there's not much of a variety."

"Water would be great," Riley said as she sat in one of the chairs taking a deep breath. "You're the only one that comes up here? You do realize this would be a great place to bring a date or impress a woman."

"Maybe that's what I'm trying to do," Alex said, eyeing Riley as she watched the stars.

Riley turned to look at Alex, she had felt a connection between them but wasn't sure that Alex felt it too. When their eyes met, she was sure.

But this wasn't Riley. She didn't hook up with random women, especially on the first night of a vacation. That's all this was, right? It had been so long since she had felt anything for another woman that she wasn't sure she could trust herself. Alex was just flirting with her, right?

Alex set the water on the table and reached for Riley's hand, slowly pulling her out of the chair. She looked into Riley's green eyes and saw all she needed to know. There was something about Riley, she'd known it when she first walked into the bar. She thought it was crazy but she felt a connection. At this moment Alex didn't want to think about that. All she wanted was to kiss the beautiful woman in front of her. She placed her other hand on the side of Riley's face and leaned in. Their lips met in a soft kiss full of possibilities. Riley put her other hand on Alex's wrist, holding it in place as they sank into the kiss.

Their lips parted briefly, but then Riley put her hands on Alex's shoulders, pulling her back in for another kiss. This one was harder. When their tongues met, Alex put her hands on Riley's hips to pull her closer. Their tongues danced and the embrace tightened until they were chest to chest and breathing hard.

As the kiss ended so they could take a breath, Alex said, "Where are my manners? I offered to make you something to eat. Let's go downstairs."

Riley smiled, not letting Alex go just yet. "Suddenly I'm not so hungry anymore, and I don't see a thing wrong with your manners."

Alex smiled back, took Riley's hand, and grabbed the bottle of water. She led them to the stairs. When they slowly walked through the bedroom, Riley couldn't help looking at the bed.

Back in the living room, Alex turned to Riley. "There's nothing I'd like more than to take you to bed, but I know you're not like that and I'm not either."

"If I'm being honest, I've never had a one night stand, and I can't believe I just told you that," Riley said covering her face with her hands.

Alex chuckled and pulled Riley's hands away, "If I'm being honest, I've never brought a woman that I just met up here."

"Really? I knew you were different."

"I'll admit I was disappointed as the night went on and you didn't come back to the bar. I thought you'd found your friend and gone back to the dock. I might have been a little excited when you walked back through the patio."

Riley raised an eyebrow. "And when you noticed that I'd missed the last ferry? Did that make you happy?"

"I wasn't mad about it." Alex laughed. "But I really did call and try to find you a room."

"I know you did. And I'll admit that I was happy when you said I could stay with you."

They smiled at one another, and their lips met again in a sweet kiss, each one dancing around the idea of being with the other.

"Have a seat." Alex pulled out a chair at the kitchen table for Riley and began laying food on the table. She had a fruit salad already cut up along with cheese, a couple of hard rolls, and some slices of turkey. "I hope this will be alright."

"It looks wonderful. I was hungrier than I thought," Riley said as she filled a plate.

"For food?" Alex said playfully.

Riley chuckled and said, "Both."

"So tell me about Riley—um, I don't even know your last name," Alex said.

"James." She paused, then said, "There's not a lot to tell."

"I don't think I know anyone named Riley."

"It was my grandmother's maiden name. My mom wanted to name me after her but, there were too many Laura's already in the family so she used her last name instead."

"That's so cool."

"How about you? I'm guessing Alex is short for Alexandria."

"You'd be right. Alex is much shorter and easier," she said looking intensely at Riley.

"Why are you looking at me like that?"

Alex laughed, "We like to play this game in the bar, guessing where people are from and what they do and why they're here. Actually, I guessed right when you and your friends walked in. I could tell you were a wedding party."

"You could?"

"Yeah. Now let's see, you have a bit of an accent, but you're tan. That tells me you're probably from the southern part of the States. I'm going to guess the Carolinas?"

"Not a bad guess, but I live in Florida. I have a bit of an accent because I lived in Texas for a while."

"Really?" Alex perked up. "That's where I'm from."

"No way. You don't have a Texas drawl," Riley said, deepening her accent.

Alex laughed. "That's pretty good. But I've been away a long time, so the accent has faded. Florida, huh? Now what do you do?" She thought for a minute and continued, "You're very helpful, watching out for your friends. You're nice or you would have told that woman hovering around you to take a hint, which she didn't. So, I'm going to say you're a nurse or a counselor. Maybe a social worker but definitely someone that helps people."

"I guess that's kind of close," Riley said. "I'm a teacher."

"Really! What do you teach?"

"Actually, I've been teaching for twenty-eight years in middle and high school, but for the last ten years I've taught language arts."

"Wow, twenty-eight years? No way! You would've had to start teaching in your teens!" Alex exclaimed.

Riley blushed. "Oh, I assure you it's been twenty-eight

years, and I am newly retired. It's time to move on to something new."

"Retired? What does that feel like?" asked Alex.

Riley thought about this for a moment, "It feels a little scary but, also exciting and full of possibilities."

"What's next?" asked Alex.

"I'm not sure. I really started thinking about it on the plane here. I've thought about writing. Now don't laugh, but I've thought about writing a book with lesbians as the main characters."

"Laugh? Why would I laugh? That's a great idea. I'd read it in a heartbeat."

"Well, at this point it's just an idea. Kara, my former best friend, and I are staying longer than the rest of the group. We're making a vacation out of the trip. Everyone else is here for a long weekend. I thought I might write down a few ideas with inspiration from the islands."

"You're staying longer than the weekend?" Alex said with hope in her voice.

"I am. Kara and I will be here for two weeks," Riley said, eyeing Alex. "You know, Kara was trying to get information out of Danny about you. She said maybe you'd show us around?"

"Danny may have said something about questions. Why did it take you so long to come talk to me?"

"Because you kept delivering drinks to our table, if you'll remember," Riley said chuckling.

Alex smiled. "Just trying to give you good service."

"Uh-huh." Riley grinned.

"I'd love to be your personal tour guide while you're here," Alex said.

"You would? I really wasn't trying to push you into anything."

"You're not. I'd like to spend more time with you. I was trying to find a way to get you to come back after the wedding," Alex admitted.

"I've been trying to figure a way to get the whole group over here tomorrow," Riley said. "They kind of owe me for leaving me behind. Not that I'm complaining."

Alex smiled and began clearing the table while Riley helped put the food away.

"I need to get a couple of things from the bedroom, I'll be right back," Alex said.

After Alex left, Riley looked out the window. She could see a few people walking on the street down below, probably heading back to their hotels for the night. She wasn't sure what was happening with Alex, but she couldn't stop thinking about that kiss on the roof. This vacation was supposed to last two weeks, and here she was in a beautiful woman's house the first night! Things like this didn't happen to Riley James. And what was this anyway? A fling? The start of something?

How could it be? She lived in Florida, and Alex was in the Virgin Islands for god's sake. Riley decided right then not to think about where this was going or what it was but to just enjoy it.

"What's so interesting out there?" Alex asked making Riley jump as she came back into the room. "Sorry, I didn't mean to startle you."

"It's okay. I was just thinking about what a day this has been."

"I brought you something to sleep in. I hope you don't mind a tank top and shorts. And I left a toothbrush on the bathroom counter for you. There are towels in the cabinet. Anything else you need?"

"Thank you. That will be perfect. I won't be too long," Riley said taking the clothes and heading to the bathroom.

"Take all the time you need." Alex could tell Riley was deep in thought when she'd walked back in the room. She couldn't believe this was happening. What was she thinking offering for Riley to stay here and then kissing her on the roof. She just couldn't help herself. There she was in the moonlight, those beautiful lips calling to her. All she wanted was to do it again. And again! She's only here two weeks, Alex thought, then she'll go back to Florida and to her life. Why not just enjoy it. It doesn't have to be anything more than what it is. A fling? The beginning of something she thought. What? There's no way Riley would want anything to do with her if she knew why Alex was on this island in the first place. Take the two weeks and enjoy being with someone.

When Riley came out of the bathroom she saw Alex tucking in a blanket on the couch. "Thanks for making up the couch. I could've done that."

"It's not for you. You're sleeping in the bed, I'm taking the couch."

"Oh, no, you're not. I can't kick you out of your bed!"

"You're my guest! You can't sleep on my couch," Alex said matter-of-factly. "Besides I want you to enjoy the view you seemed to like so much when I was showing you around. Come on." She grabbed Riley's hand and walked to the bedroom.

Once in the bedroom Alex went around to the other side of the bed. Together they pulled the bedspread and sheet back. Alex walked back around to where Riley was standing and said, "Do I need to tuck you in?"

"No... but you could stay," Riley said placing her hands on each side of Alex's face, looking into her eyes with a deep sense of want. When she saw Alex's pupils darken, she pulled her in for a kiss. The kiss deepened, and Alex's hands found their way under Riley's shirt and stroked her back. Alex moaned when she realized Riley didn't have on a bra.

The skin-to-skin contact made Riley lose her breath. It had been too long since she felt another woman's skin next to her. She sucked in and nibbled Alex's bottom lip as her tongue slid inside her mouth. As their tongues danced, Riley found the hem of Alex's tank top and pulled it over her head. Alex reciprocated, pulling Riley's shirt over her head. Riley reached behind Alex and unhooked her bra, letting it fall to the floor.

"So beautiful," Riley whispered and pulled Alex in for another searing kiss. She groaned when she felt Alex's hardened nipples touch her chest. Alex hooked her fingers into the sides of Riley's shorts and pulled them down to let her step out. She placed feather-light kisses on Riley's stomach as she worked her way back up. She stopped and took Riley's left nipple into her mouth.

"Oh god, Alex, that feels so good," Riley said as her breath quickened. Alex stood and gently pushed Riley onto the bed. She removed her own shorts and panties before she slowly lowered down next to Riley, admiring her from head to toe. She hovered for a moment looking deeply into Riley's eyes until their lips met again. Riley's left hand slid up Alex's side, leaving goosebumps in its wake, until she cupped her right breast. She lifted Alex up so she could take her breast into her mouth. She circled the nipple with her tongue as it got harder and harder, and then laid her tongue flat as the sucked it into her mouth, biting down gently.

"Good god, Riley," Alex groaned. She slid her body back down until their lips melted into one another. Alex slid her hand down Riley's side and outer thigh. When her fingers traced up the inside of her thigh, Riley bent her leg, raising her knee up and spreading her legs wider to give Alex access. Alex's hand cupped Riley's mound, and she lightly ran her middle finger from her opening up to her throbbing center. Riley was so wet it was easy for Alex to enter her.

Riley gasped and moaned Alex's name breathlessly. Alex added another finger, and Riley was in heaven. The velvet-soft wetness grabbed Alex's fingers and held them in. She started a slow rhythm that began a burning so hot in Riley she thought she'd explode. As the pace increased, Riley never wanted her to stop, but she knew she couldn't hang on much longer.

When Alex whispered "Riley" into her ear and placed her thumb right where Riley needed it, she came undone. Stars exploded behind her eyes, and when she opened them she found Alex's. They locked eye to eye. Waves of pleasure passed over Riley as she rode the orgasm out. When she finally had control of her limbs again, she kissed Alex with such tenderness that it brought tears to her eyes.

"I hope I didn't mess up your view," Alex said with a smile.

"This one is even better," Riley replied as she flipped Alex over and kissed her. "But there's more I want to see." She began kissing Alex's neck. She nibbled on her earlobe, slid her tongue in the curve of her ear, and worked her way down to her collarbone. Riley had a thing for collarbones, and Alex's were perfect. So sexy. She continued, and while she had one nipple in her mouth she pinched the other in her fingers. Alex writhed under her, moaning as her breath quickened. With both hands on her breasts, Riley kissed up and down and across Alex's stomach.

"My god, Alex, you are so beautiful," she said.

Alex ran her hands through the short red locks that

she'd been wanting to touch all night while Riley explored her body. Alex didn't think she could take much more when Riley finally made it to her center. She started at her opening and slid her tongue lightly through Alex's slick folds and circled her throbbing sex. Alex moaned again, and her hips bucked up.

"So you like that," Riley teased.

"God yes," Alex said. "Please don't stop."

Riley had no intention of stopping until Alex was a melting mess in the sheets. She tasted too good, there was no way Riley could stop. She continued circling Alex's center and eased one finger inside.

"Yes," Alex moaned.

Riley added another finger and started her own rhythm. Alex's hips started to move, but Riley held her in place, still tasting. When her rhythm increased and Alex called her name, she sucked Alex into her mouth with all she had. She felt Alex clamp down on her fingers.

"Good god, Riley!" Alex said holding Riley's head in place. Then she went limp. Riley stayed where she was for a moment then began kissing her way back up her body to her mouth. Alex could taste herself on Riley's lips.

Alex smiled weakly. "Wow!" she exhaled. "That was..."

Riley smiled back. "The view must have inspired me." She winked and settled beside Alex, who put her arm around her.

"You know I wanted to run my hands through your hair all night," Alex admitted.

Riley looked up. "You did? All night?"

Alex nodded. "Pretty much from the moment I saw you. I love red hair."

Riley smiled and ducked her head a little. "I have a thing for collarbones, and yours happen to be perfect."

"How about that. I never knew."

They both giggled.

"You said earlier that we weren't one-night-stand kind of people," Riley said. She traced her fingers in lazy circles over Alex's hipbone.

"I did."

"Well, I'm thinking that's a good thing because I'm going to need more than one night with you."

"Oh really? I did offer to be your island guide. I'm sure we could work something out that includes nights too," Alex said playfully.

"I'm liking this view more and more," Riley said.

"I'm glad you missed the boat."

"Me too," Riley said leaning in for another kiss. "But this night isn't nearly over," she said, rolling on top of Alex for more.

"Mm," purred Alex and accepted Riley's sweet lips once again.

3

Riley woke with an arm wrapped around her middle. She smiled and thought, *I could get used to this.*

But what was this? She groaned and forced herself not to think that way. She was meant to enjoy this, not think about it, overanalyze it. And how could she not enjoy it? A beautiful woman was nuzzling her neck. Riley slowly turned, smiling, and then she saw the sunrise coming through the windows and immediately sat up. "Oh Alex, it's beautiful!" she exclaimed.

Alex smiled, gazing at Riley's profile and nakedness. "It sure is."

Riley turned with a sexy smile on her face, leaned down, and gently kissed Alex. "Mm, good morning. By the way, last night was epic, as my students would say."

"Epic, huh? I'd have to agree with that," Alex said pulling her close and kissing her back. She deepened the kiss and pushed Riley down on the bed, climbing on top of her.

"Mm, what are you doing?" Riley said. "Are you trying to make me miss the ferry?"

"We have time," Alex said kissing her again. "I think after a night like last night, your day should start off epic, too." When Alex smiled, her eyes sparkled.

Riley's breath quickened. Alex kissed her way down and looked up at Riley, smiling as she stopped between her legs.

"Epic, I like that," Alex said.

"Stop talking," Riley said, putting her hands in Alex's hair.

"Bossy, I like that, too." And with that, Alex stopped talking. Riley moaned. It was an epic morning.

* * *

Riley lay on the bed, catching her breath, completely spent. "Now that's a good morning," she said with a twinkle in her eye. Alex smiled and started to get up. Riley caught her by the wrist and said, "Where do you think you're going?"

"I thought you wanted to catch the ferry," Alex said.

"I might be rethinking that. How often do they run?" Riley said with a chuckle.

"Oh, no, you don't, I'm not going to have seven lesbians hunting me down with accusations of kidnapping."

"It's not kidnapping if I'm willing. And I'm definitely a willing participant!"

"How are you so sure they'd believe that?" teased Alex.

"Oh they'd believe it, because I'm pretty sure I'll be glowing with sexual bliss all day."

"They won't give you a hard time about it, will they? Because it's not a one night stand, remember?" Alex said. Her eyes betrayed how vulnerable she was feeling.

"It'd be the best one night stand in history!" proclaimed Riley. "But no it's not. Because yes, I'm going to get on that ferry and go back to the hotel, but I'm also coming back. Today."

"Then you'd best get up. I'll go make coffee; the bathroom is yours," Alex said rolling her over and swatting her on the ass.

Riley headed to the bathroom and got into the shower while Alex quickly threw her clothes on from last night and made coffee. As she turned the hot water on, Riley noticed she couldn't stop smiling. Who smiles in the shower for no reason? But she had a reason; the more she got to know Alex the more she liked her. Kara was going to freak. She'd be surprised and happy for her, and, Riley thought as she shampooed her hair, the others will be, too. *I'm forty-nine years old, a grown woman, and retired, so at this point who cares,* she thought.

Alex filled a cup with coffee for Riley. As she neared the bathroom door she could hear Riley singing. She smiled and listened for a minute trying to recall the song, *"I've never felt like this before."* Alex had to agree, she'd never felt like this before and wondered if Riley meant it. The singing faded, so Alex knocked on the door.

"I'm leaving a cup of coffee for you on the cabinet," Alex said.

"Wow, do you give this kind of service to all the women you kidnap?"

"Only those that pretend to miss the ferry so they can seduce me."

"Seduce you! Who's seducing whom?" Riley said, sticking her head out of the shower.

"Do I need to come in there and show you?"

"I'm not stopping you," Riley challenged her.

Alex knew that if she got in the shower with her now

there'd be no way Riley would make that ferry. "No, but that damn ferry is. Let's save that for our second date." Alex winked and left the bathroom.

Hmm, second date. Riley liked the sound of that.

After brushing her teeth and towel-drying her hair, she put her clothes from yesterday back on. She changed her mind, though, and got the tank top of Alex's that she barely wore last night and put it on. She looked at her reflection in the bedroom mirror and saw something she hadn't seen in a long time. There was delight and optimism in her eyes. Sure she had a good life, and most days she was content. But spending time with Alex felt different, like there was something to look forward to. *Stop that, it's just the sex,* she thought. *Really, really good sex. Epic,* she chuckled.

As Riley walked into the kitchen she saw that Alex had toasted a couple of English muffins and had put out cream cheese and sliced fruit. There was a bottle of water sitting there for her as well as more coffee.

"This looks great. I hope you don't mind, but could I borrow your shirt to go back to the hotel? I'll bring it back later, if that's okay."

"Sure, you look better in it than I do anyway. More coffee?" Alex smiled, liking the idea of Riley wearing her shirt.

"You never told me about you last night," Riley said after a bite of English muffin. "How you got here from Texas."

Alex deflected by saying, "We were a little busy, wouldn't you say?"

Riley nodded smiling.

"Actually, I came here on vacation and never left."

"Really?"

"Yes. My best friend, Tina, and I had planned a vacation, and while I was at the airport she called and said she had a work emergency and would meet me here the next day. Her work emergency turned into a promotion, and she never made it down here."

"Wow! But why did you stay?"

"I didn't really want to do things by myself, and when I walked into Peaches I immediately hit it off with Liz. I spent a lot of time at the bar. I was unhappy in my job and Liz was looking for a bartender at the time. Long story short, I took the job, and sixteen years later I own the bar with Liz."

"That's, that's..." Riley stumbled for words.

"Crazy?"

"Actually, I was thinking brave." Riley was a little in awe of the courage it must have taken to do that. She was finding there's a lot more to Alex than bartending and rescuing strangers.

"No, it was crazy, but it's the best thing I've ever done," Alex said. "Besides helping out beautiful women that miss the ferry."

"Of course." Riley laughed along with her.

"Let me go change and I'll walk you to the dock," Alex said. She felt a bit of relief that she hadn't had to tell Riley why it was so easy to leave Texas. But what was it about Riley that made her so comfortable? For one, she didn't look down on her like so many tourists did thinking she's just a bartender. There was something about her that almost made Alex want to tell her what happened, but she couldn't chance it. Riley would be here two weeks. She should take those two weeks, show Riley around and have fun. But deep down, she already knew this wasn't a vacation fling, no matter what she tried to tell herself.

They walked down the stairs, and instead of going into the bar, they went out the back door to the beach. It was another beautiful day in paradise. A light breeze rustled the palm trees, and Riley could hear the waves lapping the sand and smell the salty air. A few birds flew overhead. It was peaceful and quiet. Riley saw a couple of people way down the beach, but no one else was around. Alex took her hand and smiled as if asking if it was okay. Riley smiled back gently, knocking their shoulders together. They walked along in silence enjoying the simplicity of the moment together.

Alex guided them onto the street that led to the dock. When they reached the dock they walked out on the pier where a few other people were waiting for the ferry. They leaned on the rail and looked out over the water. Alex pointed out a few islands in the distance and boats bobbing on the water. She pointed in the distance to the ferry that was coming toward them, getting larger every second.

"There she comes. That's your boat," Alex said.

"I have a question," Riley said. "When I bring everyone to the bar this afternoon, is it all right to walk up to you and give you a kiss?"

Alex looked into her eyes and paused, pretending to be thinking, "That would be all right only if you let me give you a kiss when you board the ferry."

"Deal," Riley said leaning over and giving her a peck on the lips. "I wouldn't want to ruin your reputation or anything," she added winking.

Alex laughed.

"Why, Alex—wait, you never told me your last name," Riley said.

"Adams, Alex Adams," she said.

"Why, Alex Adams, do you have a reputation to protect?"

"You may do whatever you want to my reputation, Riley James. I dare say being seen with you will only make it better." She grinned and gave her a peck on the lips in return.

"I swear you make me feel like a kid, Alex," Riley said, shaking her head.

Alex made the "hang loose" sign. "Epic!"

They both laughed.

Alex walked Riley onto the ferry and waved at the captain. She took her to the top deck so that Riley could look out over the island. "This is a great place to see everything. You can sit or stand and enjoy the ride."

"That's exactly what I'm doing, enjoying the ride," Riley said.

"Me too," Alex answered understanding the true meaning of Riley's words.

Alex put her hands on Riley's hips and pulled her in for a kiss. It was a sweet kiss. Longer than a simple goodbye kiss, it promised more to come.

"I've got to go. See you later today," Alex said, a little breathless as she pulled away.

"I couldn't persuade you to ride the ferry with me?" Riley said, not wanting to let her go.

"No way. Those friends may be waiting on the other shore. I'd rather you explain first," Alex said with a laugh. She walked away and turned to go down to the lower deck, though she looked back for a moment to capture Riley in her mind. She had lots of images in her mind already and knew she'd be replaying them over and over until she saw Riley again.

On the dock she waited until the ferry pulled out and then gave Riley a little wave. She waved back and then grew smaller and smaller as the ferry headed away.

* * *

Riley walked through the hotel lobby and out to their cluster of rooms. There was an area with chairs surrounded by palm trees and exotic plants that smelled even more beautiful than they looked. The chairs circled a small koi pond, which added to the beauty. It was a wonderful place to sit and enjoy the slow pace of an island morning. All of their rooms bordered this lush garden.

As Riley walked toward her room she couldn't get Alex off her mind. She had replayed their night over and over on the ferry ride back to the island. Looking out over the water she couldn't help but feel like it was calling to her. She knew how crazy it sounded, but something made her want to stay here and she knew Alex had a lot to do with it. She felt captivated. She had known this other woman for just one day! This wasn't some Lifetime movie or romance novel.

But here she was, walking to her room and thinking about Alex again. With her head in the clouds she barely noticed Kara, Kim and Kerry, and Julie and Sara sitting in the chairs watching her walk up.

"Well, look who finally made it back!" Kara said.

"Hey," Riley said with a smile.

"Nice shirt," Kara replied with questioning eyes.

Riley looked down. She had almost forgotten that she was wearing Alex's shirt. "Oh, thanks. Alex let me borrow it."

"Alex? Why did Alex lend you a shirt?" asked Kerry.

"Remember? I told you Riley was at the bar. Alex was the bartender helping her find a place to stay," Kara explained.

"Yeah, Kara, I remember, but that still doesn't explain why she lent her a shirt," Kerry said raising her eyebrows at Riley.

"She let me wear her shirt," Riley said mysteriously.

Sara said, "What are you not telling us?"

"Yeah, Riley, you look different," added Kim.

"Where did you end up staying last night anyway?" Kerry asked.

"What's with the twenty questions?" Riley said defensively.

"It's not twenty questions, we were worried about you and wondered where you got a place to stay. You didn't stay with that bartender, did you?" Sara asked.

"That bartender? Really, Sara? That bartender happens to own that bar and has a name. She's also very nice and tried to help me when my friends left me on an island," Riley said.

"It's not like we left you on purpose," Kerry said. "Where did you end up staying?"

Riley took a deep breath and said, "When we realized I'd missed the ferry, Alex called around to see if she could get me a room for the night while I tried to text Kara to see where she was. At that point I thought she was still on St. John."

Kara chimed in. "Right, we texted back and forth and realized I was here and she was there. I told you guys this last night."

"We know all that. Where did Alex find you a place to stay?" Sara asked.

"She didn't," Riley said. "The places that she would recommend were full."

"Full? The ones she'd recommend?" Kerry asked.

"Oh my god! Riley James, you had sex!" Kara jumped up and exclaimed. She ran over and pulled Riley into a bear hug. "I'm so proud of you," she said, stepping back with a smile. The others sat there with their mouths hanging open. "Say something. I want details."

Riley shook her head and couldn't stop the grin forming on her face.

"Well?" everyone said in unison.

Riley smiled from ear to ear and said, "I didn't have sex." She paused then said, "I had the most *amazing* sex!"

"Ha, I knew it! I could tell when you walked up. You were fucking glowing!" Kara said.

Kim looked at Riley with a smile, "So, spill it, what really happened?"

"She lives above the bar in the greatest apartment. It has a rooftop terrace where you can see the ocean and the stars forever. We were talking and we kissed." Riley stopped to take a breath.

"And?" Kim said prodding Riley.

"And we had something to eat, she made up the couch, and gave me this shirt to sleep in. She planned to sleep on the couch, giving me the bed."

Everyone was looking at Riley, encouraging her with their nodding heads and eyes. "Let's just say she has the most beautiful wall of windows in her bedroom that looks out over the ocean. That's all I'm telling. Oh, and I didn't sleep in this shirt. And I swear if one of you says anything or looks at me with judging eyes, you can fuck off!"

"Whoa there Riley," Kerry said holding up her hands. "We're not judging, hell I'm happy for you. How about this, we planned to take it easy this morning, have a little lunch, and check out the shops near the hotel. Then we could go back to Peaches and thank Alex for taking care of our friend?"

Riley smiled and said, "That sounds perfect to me."

"Hey Riley," Sara said, standing up, "I'm sorry if I offended you earlier. You're the one that is always looking out for us because sometimes we can be such idiots, as you well know. I can't wait to be the first to thank Alex."

"Funny, I couldn't get Alex to come back on the ferry with me this morning because she said she didn't want seven lesbians coming after her for kidnapping their friend. Looks like she may have known this group better than I thought," Riley told them chuckling.

Kara cracked, "Not sure you can kidnap the willing."

"That's what I said!" Riley laughed.

Everyone joined in the laughter. Riley sat next to Kara as the others started off on a new conversation.

"Do we need to go to our room so you can give me all the details?" Kara said twerking her eyebrows.

Riley laughed and said, "You've got all the details you're going to get from me."

"What's really going on in that head of yours?" Kara could tell something was on Riley's mind.

"I'm feeling a bit confused or overwhelmed, I'm not sure which."

"What do you mean?"

"I don't know if it's because I'm retired or the wedding or this place," she said spreading out her arms. "But I had the best time last night and can't stop thinking about her."

"You did have amazing sex, as you put it. And it's been awhile."

"Yeah, but, I can't believe I'm saying this. It felt like more than just great sex."

"What's wrong with that?"

"I don't know, it seems a bit far-fetched, doesn't it? I'm always the practical one. But here we are, on an island paradise and I sleep with someone the first night. Would you believe it if you weren't here?"

Kara chuckled, "I get it, that sounds like something I'd do. How did you leave things with her?"

"She walked me to the ferry and hoped we'd come back. It wasn't a one night stand, if that's what you're thinking."

"Of course not, you don't do one night stands."

"Oh yeah, I told her about being our guide and she was all for it."

"That tells me it might have been more than just great sex for her too."

Riley nodded hoping Kara was right.

* * *

Alex took her shoes off and walked along the beach on the way back to her place, letting the water lap over her toes. She hadn't walked the beach in a while. Sure, she ran along it sometimes on one of her morning runs, but to meander like this, it had been too long. She made a mental note to do this more often. The thought of Riley being next to her made it an even better idea.

She let her mind go and enjoyed Riley being in her thoughts. It had been so long since she'd thought of another woman that way. *Be careful, Alex,* she told herself. *Make some good memories to think back on, but don't get too attached.* That's what she'd do.

But Alex couldn't shake the conversation she'd had with Liz yesterday about Lorna. She knew Liz felt like she'd missed out not trying to make that work. Was Riley that woman for her? She felt that she was getting too far ahead of herself, but there was something about Riley. She could feel it. When she thought back on last night and those gorgeous green eyes, her heart sped up and she welcomed the cool breeze on her cheeks.

Alex got back to her place and readied for the day. When she got out of the shower she noticed Riley's shirt laying on the bed. She picked it up, held it to her face, and could smell Riley's sweet scent. It brought with it instant memories of last night and that morning, making Alex smile and her belly clinch down low. *She might not get this shirt back,* she thought.

Later she made her way to the bar to get things ready to open. She was making sure the bar was stocked, the chairs were around the tables, the porch was swept off, and the tables were wiped down, quietly singing as she did.

"Someone had a good night," Liz said as she walked over to Alex.

"Now what makes you say that?" Alex responded with a twinkle in her eye.

"Oh, the singing was a dead giveaway, but I'm not sure I've ever seen you smiling quite like that while simply wiping a table," she said and chuckled.

"Smiling quite like what?" Alex asked with a smirk on her face.

"Smiling like you did not spend the night alone in your bed," Liz stated.

Alex's cheeks reddened slightly under her tan, and she paused to look at Liz. Liz returned the look with her eyebrows raised. Then Alex laughed and said, "There's no way I could hide it, so yes, you're right, my friend. I'm saying 'my friend' so you won't tease me unmercifully all day."

Liz smiled and gave Alex a hug.

"What was that for?" Alex asked, hugging her back.

"I'm not going to tease you; I'm going to be proud of you!" Liz said happily. "Maybe you listened to me after all yesterday. And I saw the way you two were looking at one another the moment she stepped through the door."

"I'm not even going to argue with you. Riley is something special, period. I can tell," Alex said.

"Hmm," Liz pondered. "Maybe Riley has something to do with the feeling you were having yesterday morning."

"What? How could it be Riley? I didn't even know her then."

"They say love is blind," Liz commented.

"Love!? Slow down! I am going to show her around but, she's only going to be here two weeks," Alex told Liz.

"Two weeks is plenty of time. But I am happy you're actually doing something with someone else! I'll cover here for you, so take all the time you need."

Alex held up her hands. "I'm not taking off."

"You're taking some time off, and that's all there is to it." Liz held up a warning finger to cut off the protest building in Alex's throat. "Nope. Not another word about it. Now, when do you see her again?"

Alex sighed. "She's supposed to bring her group back over today sometime."

"Perfect. We'll make sure they have a good time."

Liz and Alex worked in tandem getting things ready to open. Before too long Max came in for his shift, opening the doors and welcoming the first customers. Alex went about her work greeting tourists and a few locals as the day flew by. Before long, she looked up and saw Riley and her friends enter the bar. She watched as Riley looked first at the bar and then scanned the room, looking for her. When her eyes rested on Alex, her face lit up and she walked toward her with purpose. Alex could feel her smile widening and thought she could get used to this. When Riley reached Alex she leaned up and gently placed her lips on the taller woman's and squeezed her hand.

"Hey," Riley said shyly when they broke their kiss.

"Hey back," Alex replied. Then she remembered the women behind Riley and said, "They didn't come here to hurt me, did they?"

Riley looked behind her, continuing to hold Alex's hand and said threateningly, "They'd better not."

The women stared for a moment, but then all smiled as relief washed over Alex.

A short brunette stepped up and said, "Hey Alex, I'm Kara, and on behalf of our little group here, we would like to thank you for taking such good care of our friend." She placed her hand on Riley's shoulder. "We've come to spend lots of money in your bar and have another great time. But we would also like to keep another miscommunication like yesterday from happening, though it seemed to work out pretty well for Riley. So, we would like to hang out on your patio, enjoy the beach for a bit, and then get something to eat, which we should have done yesterday, instead of continuing to drink."

She took a breath and turned back to look at her friends sternly. "After we eat we can come back and dance for a little while, but tomorrow is the wedding and no one is getting drunk tonight."

Alex looked the group over. "We can definitely take care of you on the patio, and if you'd like I'd be happy to order food that can be brought here while you enjoy the beach. There are also several food trucks right on the beach out by the patio. The music can start whenever you wish. I was happy to help out last night and give Riley a place to stay," she said, looking down at Riley with her brown eyes beaming. She caught herself then said, "Let's get y'all a table, right this way."

Riley chuckled. "I hear that Texas accent coming out."

Alex tilted her head and shrugged her shoulders. She

led them to the patio and a corner with a long table overlooking the beach. "Take this corner and enjoy. It's easy access to the beach and the food trucks are right down there," she said pointing to the trucks nearby. "There are several really good restaurants that will deliver right here, too, so if you'd rather do that, let me know. Now what's everyone drinking?"

Max walked up behind Alex and said, "I've got this, boss. Liz said for you to sit." He then addressed the group and started entertaining them with signature cocktail choices.

Alex pulled Riley aside and quietly said, "I don't want to bother you with your friends."

Riley looked at her. "Alex, you've been bothering me since you took me to that rooftop terrace of yours last night." She lowered her voice to a husky whisper and said, "And I don't want you to stop."

Alex smiled back as understanding reached her eyes, darkening them and coloring her cheeks.

"I hope I'm not interrupting, but would you like a drink?" Max asked Riley.

"I think I could use one to cool off a little," she said looking at Alex with the most vibrant green eyes.

"Hey Alex," someone yelled, tearing her away from those eyes she was falling into. She turned, and it was Sara asking her which food truck had the best tacos. Alex smiled and went over to point out the one she liked. They welcomed her into the group, asking questions about the bar and the islands. She entertained them with funny tourist stories. Some of Riley's friends walked on the beach, others played in the surf as the waves came in, and Alex and Riley were rarely apart. It was obvious they were drawn to each other, and the group didn't seem to mind at all. Alex ordered seafood and had it delivered on the patio as the afternoon turned into twilight.

As she cleared away some of the plates to make room for more drinks, Kim and Kerry followed her into the bar. She set the dishes down behind the bar, and Kim said, "Hey Alex, could we have a minute?"

"Sure," Alex said. "Can I get you something else?"

"Gosh no, this has been a really fun day for everyone. Thanks for doing that, but Kerry and I wanted to first thank you again for taking care of Riley. She's really important to us, and we panicked when we realized what had happened."

"It was no problem. It can be scary when you realize you've missed that ferry. I've gotten stuck a few times over on St. Thomas myself," Alex answered.

"Actually we'd like to invite you to our wedding tomorrow," Kerry said. "We know it's short notice, but we'd really like it if you could be there."

Alex didn't know what to say.

"We'll understand if you don't want to—I mean, you just met us and all—but you fit right in with our group. I know Riley would like it, and we would, too," Kim added. "What do you say?"

"Well," Alex said, her face brightening, "that sounds like so much fun, but let me ask Riley first."

"Ask Riley what?" Riley said, walking up to the bar. She looked between Alex and Kim and Kerry.

"We invited Alex to the wedding tomorrow, but she wanted to check with you first."

Riley's face lit up. "That sounds wonderful. Can you come? I'd love for you to be there. But only if you're my date, it could be our second," she said with a wink.

"In that case I'd love to. Thanks so much for inviting me."

"Okay, now that we have that settled, let's turn that music up, I want to dance with my girlfriend one more night before she gets married. Maybe I'll get lucky," Kim said wiggling her eyebrows up and down.

Kerry pulled Kim into her arms with a laugh. "I love you! I'm so glad we're finally getting married." She planted a sweet kiss on her lips, then dragged her onto the dance floor.

"I like those two," Alex said, smiling as they left.

Riley nodded. "They were made for one another."

"And how nice to invite me to their wedding. Are you sure you're okay with that?"

Riley placed her hands on each side of Alex's hips, pulling her close. "I'm more than okay with it." She kissed Alex, long and slow, weakening her knees. When their lips parted she whispered breathlessly, "I've been wanting to do that since I walked in this bar and saw those beautiful brown eyes."

She took Riley's hand and whisked her through a door at the end of the bar. When the door closed Alex pushed her against it. She looked into Riley's green eyes and saw her pupils darkening as she placed her hands on either side of her face. She leaned down and crushed Riley's lips with her own. A moan escaped Riley as she grabbed Alex and pulled her closer. Alex wedged her leg between Riley's and thrust her tongue in her mouth. If Riley hadn't been holding on to Alex she would have slid down the wall. They were both panting when they broke for air. Neither said a word as their mouths met again, and Alex moaned as Riley grabbed her ass with both hands. Before those hands could roam any farther, Alex broke the kiss and met Riley's forehead with her own.

"I've been wanting to do that since I put you on that ferry this morning," she said.

They smiled at one another, unspoken words in their eyes, questions, hopes, lust. Was it just lust? Two weeks would tell.

Alex took a deep breath. "We've got to get back out there before your friends turn on me."

"Okay, but that was one epic kiss," Riley said, winking.

Alex chuckled. "It sure was!"

4

It wasn't long until they had to catch the ferry back and get ready for Kim and Kerry's big day. Everyone thanked Alex for the special treatment and headed to the dock. Alex wanted to walk with Riley to steal a few minutes alone. Liz told her things would be fine until she got back. As they walked hand in hand at the back of the group Alex said, "I know this sounds strange, but I can't wait to see you tomorrow. I wish you could stay."

"That doesn't sound strange to me because I wish I could stay, too. I tell you what, when you come for the wedding tomorrow evening, plan to stay with me this time. I mean, if you want to?" Riley said, hoping she didn't sound pushy. She didn't know what was happening, but she wanted to be with Alex all the time. This was crazy. It was so fast. She'd certainly never felt like this so quickly before. *Maybe it's the island air,* she thought.

"That's a great idea," Alex said playfully. "Then last night wouldn't be a one night stand. It'd be a first night stand." She laughed and bumped Riley's shoulder. "How stupid did that just sound?"

Riley laughed, too. "That didn't sound stupid at all. I think it was sweet. You're trying to save my reputation." She bumped Alex's shoulder back. They walked in silence enjoying being together for a bit before Riley said, "You know, you can come over early tomorrow if you want. Just text me."

"It depends on how busy we are tomorrow afternoon. I'll see what I can do, though. Otherwise I'll meet you at the hotel."

"I'll be waiting on you."

They made their way to the dock, and while the others got on the ferry and walked up to the top deck, Riley pulled Alex under the stairway and put her arms around her neck. She looked into Alex's whiskey-brown eyes. They filled her with such longing, and neither said a thing.

Alex smiled and gently brought their lips together in a sweet good night kiss. "Sweet dreams, Riley," she whispered. The warning horn sounded, and Alex pulled away to leave the ferry.

Riley was in a daze as she climbed the steps to the top deck. She looked back at where they boarded, and there was Alex, smiling and waving. She watched as Alex took out her phone and started texting. In a moment Riley's phone pinged in her pocket.

Alex: This is twice today I've put you on a ferry going away from me. I don't like it.

Riley: Just so you know, I don't like it either. Kindly tell me what's happening to us.

Riley wasn't sure if she should text that, but this was all so confusing and wonderful at the same time. She thought she knew herself better than this and was so surprised at what she was feeling and doing. Having great sex had turned her into a person she didn't know yet wanted to be. She liked this carefree, constantly smiling, hand-holding and bartender-kissing person that Alex had found in her.

Alex: I don't know but I like it. And I hope it keeps happening over and over and over!

Riley: Me too!

When Riley looked up she waved, but Alex had disappeared in the distance. She sighed.

Alex walked back to the bar and couldn't remember when she'd felt like this. She couldn't wait for tomorrow and the day with Riley.

"I love that happy look on your face," Liz said as Alex came around the bar.

"I like how it feels, but it's also terrifying," Alex admitted. "I don't know what's happening, Liz. I feel such a connection to Riley, and I know she feels it too. How can that be when I've only known her for one day?"

"I'm sure it is terrifying, Alex, but don't run," Liz said in a stern voice.

"That's just it, I don't want to run. I want to see what happens, if there's a chance for something. But then, I remember," she said, her voice dropping, tinged with sadness. "I remember how I got here and why I'm alone."

"Stop! That was a long time ago. Put it out of your mind and go explore with Riley. Find out what this might be, and we'll worry about the past later," Liz said stepping in front of Alex and looking into her eyes. "Be happy, Alex. Try it on for a while, live in it."

Alex took a deep breath and let it out. "This goes against everything I know I should do, but okay. I'm going to let it go for now and find out more about Riley James." Alex smiled. "Thanks, Liz."

"Anytime, sweetie."

* * *

The next day, Riley and Kara sat next to one another in the hotel's spa. Kim and Kerry were excited for the ceremony that evening and had treated the group to a mini spa day with manis and pedis in the morning. They were in the middle of their pedicures when Kara looked over at Riley thoughtfully.

"So what's going on? You look so serious."

Riley looked over at Kara. "I was just thinking."

"About what? It wouldn't be a beautiful bartender, would it?"

"She is beautiful, isn't she?" Riley said wistfully and smiling. "I can't get her out of my head."

"Why would you? You two click."

"What do you mean?" Riley asked.

"It's obvious. When you two aren't making goo-goo eyes, you can tell how comfortable you are with each other. You click. It's like you should be together."

"Really?"

"Yeah, you two don't seem to see it, but it's obvious. The question you should ask is, is she in your heart?"

"I know," Riley answered. "Believe me I've asked that and the answer is 'How could she be, when we haven't known each other that long?'"

"So what!" Kara exclaimed. "Who says you have to know someone a specific amount of time before you let them in your heart? Who says you have to date someone for so many months before you go to the next step? You don't let society dictate your life or you wouldn't be the successful, openly gay teacher that you are. If she's in your heart, why not let her live there?"

Riley sighed. "Because when you let someone in your heart, that's when you get hurt."

"It is, but you also get to love and be loved. That's the best feeling there is."

"But what if Alex doesn't feel the same way?"

Kara said, "Well, obviously I don't know Alex very well, but I can see how she looks at you. There is more than lust in her eyes. I see the connection you two have. Why not see where it goes? Nobody says you have to go home after two weeks. If you'll remember, you're retired."

Riley said, "I know, I've been thinking the same thing."

"Then quit thinking and just enjoy."

* * *

Alex walked into the hotel bar and sat at a table near the entrance. She was wearing a linen pair of pants with wide legs that flowed when she walked and a sleeveless top to match. Her sandals were flats that would be perfect for a beach wedding. She laid her small overnight bag at her feet as she got out her phone.

Alex: I'm in the bar.
Riley: On my way.

Alex smiled and shook her head as she read the text thinking how much she'd missed Riley last night. And this morning she couldn't get Riley off her mind. She finally gave up and got her things ready for this evening. When she looked up, Alex lost her breath.

Riley was standing in the entrance to the bar looking for her. She had her short locks styled in sassy, red curls. Her long dress had a subtle pastel print with spaghetti straps that accentuated her toned and tanned shoulders. Alex couldn't wait to slide those straps down and slowly kiss her shoulder, making her way up to her neck.

Then Riley found her. Their eyes met, and the smile on Riley's face brightened the room. That's when Alex knew she was a goner. In such a short time Riley James had captured her heart. She could fight this feeling, but she knew it was a losing battle. All Alex could do was hope that Riley wanted her heart and wouldn't break it.

Riley walked toward Alex, and her eyes widened. She took her hands and said, "You look beautiful!"

"No, you look stunning," Alex said, breathlessly placing a kiss on Riley's cheek. They looked into one another's eyes, and both took a deep breath and sighed.

Riley laced her fingers through Alex's hand. "Come on." She pulled her through the door, out the lobby, and onto the walkway toward their cluster of rooms. On the left was a bench. Riley sat down pulling Alex beside her and putting her arm around her shoulders.

"I want you all to myself for a minute before we meet the others," Riley said.

"Oh, you do?"

Their eyes met, and they stared, relaying unspoken emotions. Alex leaned in, giving Riley a sweet kiss. When their lips parted, Riley smiled into Alex's lips and kissed her again, deeper this time.

"Mm, that will have to get me through until later," she said a little breathlessly.

"Hey, what are you two doing?" Kara yelled as she walked toward them.

They looked at one another with guilty smiles. "Who, us?" Alex said.

Kara laughed. "I've come to take you to the beach. Let's get this wedding started!"

They got up and all walked down the path past their rooms and out to the beach. The rest of the group was there, including someone new with Lee and another woman Riley didn't know. She asked Kara, "Hey, who's that?"

Kara replied, "That's my date for the wedding, and if she's good, I may let her hang around after."

"You're terrible," Riley said. Alex smiled and shook her head. "Do you know her?" Riley asked Alex.

"I do. She grew up here and works on one of the day boats. She comes in the bar occasionally," Alex answered.

Riley narrowed her eyes, not quite sure Alex was telling her everything. "Uh-huh," she murmured.

"Okay, there might have been one night that she drank a little too much and decided I was going home with her," Alex said.

"Well, don't stop there... And?"

"And I said she decided, but not me. I politely declined and made sure she made it home alright. She's been back in the bar since and was embarrassed, and that's the end of the story."

"Hmmm, I see," Riley said looking the woman up and down.

"What are you doing? Why, Riley James, don't tell me you're jealous?"

"Jealous! How could I be jealous?" Riley said defensively.

Alex raised her eyebrows.

"Okay, I might have been a little, but honestly I don't know where that came from," Riley confessed.

Alex chuckled. "You're kind of cute when you're jealous. And I bet you're downright adorable when you're mad, but I don't really want to find that out tonight."

Riley looked down sheepishly and took Alex's hand, putting her head on her shoulder.

"It's okay, Riley," Alex said, putting her arm around her waist. "You know that first day you came in the bar and Lee kept hovering around you?"

"Yeah, of course I remember."

"I didn't like it one little bit and I hadn't even met you yet," Alex admitted. "I was trying to come up with a reason for you to come back to the bar with me so she'd leave you alone. Next thing I knew, there you were asking me to mix you a pretend drink."

"Best move I ever made," Riley said proudly.

"I'm so glad you did."

"Do you mean if I hadn't come up there you would have found a way to get me alone and introduce yourself?" Riley asked.

"I kept telling you my name every time I came to your table! And yes, I would've found a way."

"Alex Adams, you little charmer," Riley said.

Alex shrugged her shoulders and smiled.

Kara had made her way over to them and introduced her date.

"Riley, Alex, this is Mandy. Mandy, my best friend, Riley, and her new friend, Alex."

Riley extended her hand. "Hi Mandy, nice to meet you." To Kara she said, "New friend?"

"Hi Riley," Mandy said, taking her hand. "And I know Alex. How are you? I haven't been to Peaches in a while."

"I'm good, really good," Alex said looking at Riley. "Peaches is good, too. Come by sometime."

"I'm sure we'll be over there again soon since you've charmed my friend. She can't go a day without her Peaches fix," Kara said.

Riley looked at Kara and shook her head.

"Would you take your seats? We're ready to begin," Lisa announced. She was the officiant and stood under an arch laced with fragrant flowers. The sun was beginning to set and cooperated with a beautifully lit sky with reds and oranges that would change to shades of purple by the end of the ceremony.

Kim and Kerry made their way down the aisle between the chairs set up on the beach hand in hand. They looked lovely in pale, lemon-colored outfits. Kim chose a skirt just below knee length with a loose-fitting camisole that flowed below her waist. Kerry was in wide leg pants with a flowing, three-quarter-sleeve blouse.

This ceremony was just for their close friends that had been with them from the beginning. Their families would all be in attendance at a separate reception later in the month.

Lisa started the ceremony, and as Kim and Kerry began to exchange vows Alex had an unexplainable need to touch Riley. She reached over and took Riley's hand and held it in her lap. She stole a sideway glance at Riley and saw tears glistening in her eyes.

Riley didn't know why she was tearing up. She didn't cry at weddings, but for some reason the tenderness of the moment watching Kim and Kerry stand there making promises to one another shot straight to her heart. She'd never thought marriage was for her, but in this moment she thought that maybe she was wrong. How wonderful it must be to stand there in front of family and friends and proclaim your love and promise to live life together, to live your love. She was glad Alex took her hand and held it close. It steadied her and calmed these thoughts racing through her mind and heart.

Lisa introduced the Mrs. and Mrs. to applause and whoops of congratulations. The ceremony was touching in a beautiful setting and full of love. The beach party to follow was just getting started.

As evening turned into night there was good food, music, and laughter. Couples twirled on the makeshift dance floor. Alex looked across the beach and saw Riley with Kim and Kerry. Riley threw her head back laughing, and Alex's heart skipped a beat. *She is so beautiful,* Alex thought. When Riley looked her way and their eyes met, Alex couldn't keep from smiling. She went to her and took her hand.

"Would you dance with me?" Alex asked.

"I'd love to."

A slow song started, and Riley wrapped her arms around Alex's neck, looking into her eyes. Alex had her hands around Riley's waist and pulled her close. She bent down and placed a kiss on Riley's shoulder.

"I've wanted to do that all night. You are absolutely gorgeous."

Riley took a deep breath and said, "You do know how to charm a girl."

"I actually can't wait to get you out of this dress later tonight."

"Is that so?"

"You did ask me to stay the night with you, remember?"

"I seem to remember something like that, since you so kindly let me stay at your place," Riley answered. "Let me warn you that it won't have the view yours has, though."

"There's no better view than the one I have right now," Alex said, watching Riley's eyes darken.

Riley gazed into Alex's eyes longingly, then said, "We'd

better talk about something else before I take you straight to my room and lock the door. Kim and Kerry might find that rude since I'm here for their wedding."

Alex smiled. "Understood. So, let's see, have you ever wanted to get married?"

Riley said, "Well, I never really thought marriage was for me, but after today I might have to reconsider. But to answer your question, no, I've never wanted to get married. I seem to have a three-year expiration date."

Alex looked puzzled. "A three-year expiration date? What does that mean?"

"Well, I've had three separate relationships that each lasted about three years. I don't know what happens, but three years and it's over. What about you?"

"So, if I still know you after three years, then there's hope?"

Riley furrowed her brow. "Hope? Then this would turn into the longest one night stand in history! But you didn't answer my question. Have you ever wanted to get married?"

"Sorry, I was distracted by your three-year expiration date thing. But no, I have never wanted to get married. Honestly, and I can't believe I'm telling you this, I haven't had a relationship long enough to even think about it. How big of a loser does that make me?"

"That doesn't make you a loser at all." Before Riley could say more Kim asked for everyone to gather round for a toast. Alex was relieved because she certainly didn't want to talk about her past.

After a few toasts there was more dancing and laughter as the group celebrated the brides into the night. When the brides declared the honeymoon was beginning, Riley quickly finished her drink, said goodnight to her friends, and pulled Alex off the beach and onto the path to her room.

Neither one of them spoke on the short walk. Riley opened the door and went in. As soon as Alex cleared the doorway, Riley shut it behind them and pushed Alex against it all in one move. Her lips landed where they'd wanted to be since she'd kissed Alex on the bench earlier. While her hands found their way under Alex's shirt, she put her knee between those long, muscular legs, and Alex groaned. They both moaned as their tongues connected and explored.

Their lips parted so they both could breathe. Alex gently lowered the straps of Riley's dress. She kissed her left shoulder, making her way across to the hollow of her throat and licking and nipping her way across to the other shoulder.

Riley moaned, "Oh Alex." She looked into Alex's darkening eyes questioning, seeking approval. Alex nodded with fire in her eyes, and Riley lifted her shirt over her head and tossed it on the floor. She smiled when she saw Alex wasn't wearing a bra. She placed her hands on the waistband of Alex's pants and pulled them and her panties down in one motion. Her lips found Alex's as she turned, pushing her gently to the bed. When the backs of her knees found the mattress, Riley pushed her down.

"You're the most beautiful woman I've ever seen, Alex."

Alex smiled and said, "You have on way too many clothes."

Riley quickly took her dress off and slowly unhooked her bra. She slid her panties down her legs, giving Alex a little show.

"You're beautiful," Alex said, her breath quickening. Riley stepped between Alex's legs, placing her knees on the bed, her hands on either side of Alex's head, and lowered her lips to Alex's. She kissed her way down to Alex's left nipple, swirling her tongue around and taking the hardening bud into her mouth. Alex moaned and arched her back.

"I can't leave this other beautiful bud out," she said, so she kissed her way to the other nipple while taking the left between her thumb and finger and pinching it softly. She continued her way to Alex's stomach, nipping and licking while raking her fingernails through Alex's short, curly hair. Alex pushed the back of her head into the bed and raised her hips. Riley hovered over Alex's sex and said, "Alex, look at me."

Alex raised her head as her heart pounded and breath came quickly, seeking Riley's eyes. When she found them, Riley gently slid one finger in, never breaking eye contact. She added a second finger, then slowly went in and out. Alex's eyes closed momentarily then opened, pleading with Riley. She buried her head between Alex's legs and circled her tongue around and around. Alex grabbed Riley's head and moaned, "Oh, god!"

This exquisite rhythm continued and it wasn't long before Riley could feel Alex tighten around her fingers and thrust them in and upward and left them there as she sucked Alex into her mouth. Her legs began to quake and her hips bucked as Riley's tongue was relentless. Her legs stiffened as the orgasm overtook her, but Riley didn't stop. Her mouth continued its magic as Alex came again. Alex flung her arms out on the bed, her legs relaxed as she lay spent. Riley laid her head on the inside of Alex's thigh.

"There are no words," Alex said. She raised her head and looked down at Riley. "Come here." She put her hands under Riley's chin and pulled her toward her and kissed her softly. She put Riley's head on her chest while her breath recovered then said, "That was, was... well, pick an adjective."

Riley chuckled, raising her head to rest it in her hand. "Um, mind-blowing."

"Exactly," Alex grinned. After a moment she continued, "I swear, Riley, I've never..." She found she couldn't finish the sentence.

Riley smiled and said, "I was really inspired."

Alex smiled, turned Riley on her back, and said, "I hope you got plenty of sleep last night because I'm about to show you how inspired I am. I'm going to show you over and over and over."

* * *

Alex stood in front of the bathroom sink putting her hair in a ponytail.

Riley walked up and encircled her waist from behind. "What a wonderful night."

"It sure was," Alex purred, leaning back into Riley's embrace.

Their eyes met in the mirror. Riley had her chin on Alex's shoulder and said, "Coffee, I need coffee. The others will be at the circle, let's go."

Alex asked, "The circle?"

"That's what we call the gathering spot outside our rooms. Kim and Kerry will be leaving soon, so we're meeting up to tell them goodbye." They faced one another, and Riley gave Alex a quick kiss while cupping Alex's face with her right hand. "I can't seem to keep my hands off of you."

Alex smiled, leaning into Riley's hand, and said, "I hope that doesn't change."

"I can't imagine anything that would do that," Riley said. "Come on, let's go."

Alex thought to herself that she knew something that could change that but hoped Riley wouldn't find out.

They joined the others at the circle. Everyone got something to drink and talked about how wonderful the wedding was. Alex was standing off to the side listening to the chatter when Sara walked up.

"You two seem to really be getting along," she said.

Alex nodded her head. "We are."

"I can't help but notice how you two seem to fit together in such a short time."

Alex looked at Sara warily and said, "It's surprising to us, too, but we've agreed to just enjoy it and stop questioning it."

"That's all good, but I can't imagine how this is going to end in two weeks. I'm not trying to be an asshole, Alex. Riley is my friend, and I don't want her to get hurt," Sara explained.

"I understand, but you need to know I'd never hurt Riley. I don't see this as a vacation fling if that's what you're getting at."

"That's quite a statement for only knowing one another a few days. I'm sure you're aware of that."

"I am."

Riley called out to them. "Come on, Kim and Kerry are leaving now." As they walked over to her Riley looked at Alex and noticed she seemed unsettled. She made a mental note to ask her later what she and Sara had been talking about.

They all took turns hugging Kim and Kerry and walked them to the lobby. They were continuing their honeymoon through the islands while most of the group was leaving to go back to Florida. Riley and Kara had planned to change hotels but stay for their two extra weeks. After discussing their options they decided to go back to St. John with Alex and find a place there. Alex had agreed to be their tour guide, so it would be easier if they all stayed near her.

Riley couldn't help smiling as she threw clothes into her bag. It was shaping up to be a great vacation.

5

Later that evening Riley walked into Peaches like she owned the place. She sat down at the bar right in front of Alex and placed her hands on the top with a smack.

Alex smirked and said, "Well, what can I get you, ma'am?" Her eyes twinkled in the low light.

"How about one of those exquisite kisses of yours," Riley demanded.

Alex laughed and looked at her, then leaned over the bar and gave her what she wanted.

Riley said, "I've always loved the service in this bar."

Alex shook her head. "Did you and Kara get moved into your new hotel?"

"We did. Thanks for arranging all that for us."

"You're very welcome. We take service seriously here at Peaches," Alex played along.

"I know you do," Riley said rather seductively.

"Okay, okay, that's enough from the hot lovers. This is a business, if you'll remember, and we do have other customers," Liz said playfully.

"And all of those customers are enjoying their drinks if you will notice, Liz."

Ignoring Alex, Liz said, "Riley, Alex said you and your friend moved over here for the rest of your stay and she is adding tour guide to her duties."

"I hope that's all right, Liz. Kara and I were looking forward to Alex showing us around. You know, giving us a look at real island life."

"Uh-huh, I'm sure that's what you were looking for, Riley," Liz said with a smirk.

"Where is Kara anyway?" Alex said, changing the subject.

"She met up with Mandy when she finished work this evening, so it's just me tonight. I would be glad to help out around here."

"That's nice of you, but we have plenty of help. Sunday night is usually quiet because the vacationers have gone home and the next groups arrive on Monday. I've got an idea: have you been for a sunset walk on the beach since you got here?" Liz asked.

"You know, I haven't."

"Well, tonight would be the perfect night for that. Alex, get out of here."

"Wait, Liz," Riley objected. "Alex was off last night for the wedding. I was going to hang here until she was finished tonight. I don't want to get in the way."

"You're not in the way. It's a beautiful evening, and there's going to be a spectacular sunset. You two go! For me."

"Don't try to argue with her. When she makes up her mind it's done," Alex said coming around the bar. "I'll be right back." She disappeared through the door to her place upstairs.

Liz grabbed a small insulated bag and put a few beers

into it. She came around the bar and put the bag on Riley's shoulder. "This will make it a lot more fun!" she said and winked at Riley. "Just so you know, Alex doesn't do this. I mean, she never walks on the beach with someone. I think you have charmed her, Riley, and hope you continue to do so. Don't you worry about her taking time off, I'll take care of it." Liz put her arm around Riley and squeezed her shoulder. They looked at one another, nodding as if an agreement had been reached.

Alex came in with a small bag over her shoulder. "Ready to go?" she asked, offering her hand to Riley.

Riley took her hand. "Lead the way."

Liz watched them leave, smiling and thinking to herself that Riley was just what Alex needed. Somehow they were going to find a way to be together. She knew that as sure as she knew that sunset was going to be beautiful. There was no way she was going to let Alex mess this up. She was even determined to work a little island magic if needed. Liz had known her for a long time now, and she'd never seen her look at another woman the way she looked at Riley.

They walked hand in hand along the beach away from all the bars and people. Alex stopped at a little place where the beach began to curve. It was a small shelter, more like a three-sided lean-to, that had seen better days. Alex spread a towel out in front of it, making a perfect spot to watch the sun set. As night fell they would be secluded from anyone walking this far down the beach. Riley set the bag down with the beer, and Alex began to bring out cheese, bread, and fruit for an impromptu picnic.

"Have a seat. I threw a few things together, but I'll take you on a real picnic soon," Alex said sitting next to Riley.

"This is perfect," Riley said opening each of them a beer. The sun was just above the horizon, beginning the show.

The fiery orange gave way to muted reds, and as it inched down the sky, it turned from the most beautiful purple to deep violet. They were afraid to look away in case they missed another color. A few early stars were coming out above them.

They nibbled on the snacks and finished their beer as they sat in comfortable silence. It seemed they were always touching, whether it was hands brushing while they shared the food or legs touching while they sat and soaked up the beauty. As night began to fall, Riley sat back on her elbows and looked at the stars above them. The water gently washed ashore in a quiet melody accompanying the show above. Riley thought this was the most romantic moment she'd ever lived.

She sat up and put her arm around Alex's waist and her head on her shoulder. "This must be what heaven is like."

Alex smiled. "It is beautiful. I've lived here a long time, but this is one of the best sunsets I've ever seen. I think it's because of who I'm with." She turned and looked deeply into Riley's eyes. She took her face in her hands and kissed her. When their lips met Alex felt her heart open and a flood of emotions came rushing out. Riley deepened the kiss, taking the emotions that flowed from Alex. The feelings slammed into Riley's heart, taking her breath and jolting her heart into overdrive. This was different. This wasn't a kiss filled with lust and sex to come. This was a kiss full of hope, as if their hearts were exchanging the feelings they were afraid to admit with their heads simply because it was too soon.

They pulled back and looked into one another's eyes. Alex gently ran the backs of her fingers down Riley's cheek and sighed. Right now words were not needed. They both felt the shift from "just enjoy it" to something more between them.

Riley was trying to process what had just happened but ended the moment by whispering, "I told Kara I would see her at the hotel tonight." Even though she said it, there was such longing in her eyes.

Alex nodded. "That's actually a good thing. You'll need a good night's sleep to be ready for the adventure we're planning tomorrow. And you won't get much sleep if you stay with me."

Riley arched an eyebrow while putting her arms around Alex's neck. "Is that so?"

Alex chuckled. "You know it is. I can't keep my hands off of you either."

Riley agreed and said suggestively, "But I don't have to go back just yet. Sitting on the beach, making out with a hot bartender after a killer sunset sounds like a nice night." She pulled Alex close and kissed her. "I don't think I'll ever tire of kissing these lips," she said her lips on Alex's.

"Then don't stop." And they didn't.

Alex walked Riley back to her hotel, hand in hand.

"What exactly are we doing tomorrow, tour director?"

Alex laughed. "I'm not exactly a tour director, and I say that now because I don't want you to expect too much. We may not exactly do what tourists do; however, tomorrow we're going out on the boat Mandy works on to snorkel and kayak."

"That's like tourists."

"Yes, but the rest of the time probably won't be, if that's all right."

"That's fine. I want you to show me your island, your paradise."

They'd reached Riley's door. Alex turned to her and said

softly, "I'd love for you to be part of my paradise." She leaned down and kissed her softly.

"Mm, are you sure it's a good idea for me to stay here tonight?" Riley moaned.

"No, but I think you'd better," Alex said, her forehead on Riley's. "You and Kara meet me at the restaurant across from the bar for breakfast, and we can walk to the boat. Wear something to swim in and don't forget sunscreen. I can't have this beautiful body of yours burned."

"Burned? You keep me burning all the time!"

Alex smiled and placed a chaste kiss on Riley's lips. "Good night, Riley. See you in the morning." Alex started to walk off.

"You know how to break a girl's heart, Alex Adams."

"Aww, don't say that," Alex said, stopping. "I'll mend it tomorrow."

Riley grabbed her hand, gave her a gentle kiss, and said, "You just did. Thank you for a wonderful evening."

"My pleasure."

Riley opened the door and winked, "See you tomorrow, beautiful." Alex smiled and walked away. Riley watched her as her heart swelled with affection. Sure, she liked Alex, but she also knew it was much more than that. She had that fluttery feeling in her stomach. She knew what it meant but was afraid to admit it just yet.

On the walk back home Alex didn't know when she'd felt so light and happy. It had been quite some time—in fact, she couldn't remember when the last time had been. Not that she was unhappy, but here she was, walking home, smiling for no reason. Well, she knew the reason, Riley James.

What had started out as a vacation fling with a nice

person had somehow morphed into more than that. She wasn't ready to actually say the word or believe what was happening, but when she thought back to that kiss on the beach, the one where she felt like she was being transported straight into Riley's heart, it was like she could see something forming in the distance, a glow gathering brightness that was filling Riley's heart and spilling out, searching, until it found Alex. It slammed into Alex's heart and filled her to overflowing. She couldn't think, see, or hear anything but this wonderful warmth surrounding her heart, holding it close and not letting go. When the kiss had ended and they'd looked into one another's eyes, it was as if their hearts were speaking to one another in a language only they knew. Their hearts already knew what their minds were afraid to believe.

Alex took a deep breath, feeling as if she'd just run a marathon. That was a lot to take in to think about and work out. She decided not to, not right now anyway. All she wanted to do was soak up the warmth that Riley had surrounded her with and give it right back to her. She couldn't wait until tomorrow.

* * *

After breakfast Alex, Riley, and Kara were on their way to the dock when Kara asked, "So, what do you know about Mandy, Alex?"

"What do you mean? Haven't you spent the last two days with her?"

"Yes, but you know what I mean. Is she a serial killer or anything like that?"

Alex laughed. "What is it with you two and serial killers?"

"I asked Alex the same thing when I got stuck over here that first night," Riley explained.

"Mandy comes from a good family," Riley said. "She grew up here in the islands. She went off to college and came back. She loves what she does on the tour boat, and I don't think it will be long until she's running her own. Let's see, as far as I know she has not killed anyone and is a nice person."

"What do you care anyway?" Riley asked. "I thought you were having a vacation island fling."

"I am, unlike two people I know holding hands as we walk to the boat," Kara said looking at Riley, then Alex with humor in her eyes. "I know she's younger than me, and I guess I was just wondering about her. Does that make me a cougar?"

"Of course it does! You're the hottest cougar in Florida, so why wouldn't you be in the Virgin Islands, too?" Riley said.

Alex laughed. "No offense, Kara, but I might have to disagree with that statement."

Riley looked at her and said, narrowing her eyes, "Just how old are you, Alex?"

"I'm forty-six, Riley, your age! I was just kidding."

"How do you know how old I am?"

"I heard you tell one of your friends you were turning fifty. And I didn't believe it, by the way."

"Well, thank you."

"Hey, look, there's Mandy," Kara said, excitedly waving to her. "I think we're about to get the VIP treatment. Look at that boat! This is going to be great!"

Mandy welcomed them all onto the boat. She introduced them to the captain and other mates. They walked around checking out the boat while the other people boarded.

"Come with me, I'll show you a good place to sit because we'll be shoving off soon," Mandy told them. She led them to a good spot where they could see the mates working the sails. The captain told stories as they sailed out into the aquamarine sea. The sails filled with wind, and they flew across the water, the wind whipping through their hair.

The first stop was in the Caribbean Sea for snorkeling. Mandy was the first mate on this voyage and gave everyone instructions on how to use the equipment, clearing their masks, using the snorkel and fins, so that even a beginner would feel comfortable.

"Let's pair up, and I'll help you descend to the water," said Mandy. "Once we're all in the water I'll show you some great places to explore."

After following Mandy they were given free time to explore on their own. Alex took Riley to an area full of brightly colored fish, and they even saw a sea turtle.

"Don't forget to watch out for jellyfish," Alex reminded Riley. At one point Alex looked ahead, and a jellyfish about the size of her hand was floating her way. She simply swam to the right and let it go by. It didn't try to bother Alex, and she certainly didn't want to bother it.

Alex watched the jellyfish as it continued past her and was struck by the fact that, in the last eighteen years, this was how she treated most people. The people she came into contact with were beautiful to watch passing through her life, but she always got out of the way, afraid they would sting her. All these years she had kept a secret inside, afraid to tell anyone, because of shame and the fear of disgust if they knew what she had done.

But Alex felt different now. She didn't want to always be

swimming away. What if she took the chance and told someone? What if they didn't sting her and didn't feel disgust? Liz was always telling her to give people a chance; after all, she still loved her and she knew. Alex decided right then that she was going to tell Riley what she'd been keeping inside all these years. She didn't know when she'd tell her, but before Riley left to go home, Alex was going to take a chance.

"If you would make your way back to the boat, please," Mandy shouted to the group. The boat was noisy as everyone excitedly shared with their friends what they had seen. After putting the equipment away and settling in for the next sail, Alex got them all a drink and sat next to Riley, grabbing her hand. Riley smiled at her as just this simple touch made her heart swell.

Mandy told them facts and stories about the islands and pointed out landmarks as they made their way to a small, uninhabited beach and lowered the anchor. The water was shallow, and as they left the boat they waded ashore where a lunch feast awaited them. There were several kinds of fish, fruits, and other treats, as well as plenty to drink.

Alex, Riley, and Kara filled their plates and found a place on the beach to eat and relax. After all the passengers had their food and were seated, Mandy came and joined them.

"This is incredible," Kara told Mandy as she sat down beside her.

"I'm glad you're having a good time."

"I couldn't believe all the fish we saw," Riley said.

"Are those pirate stories that you were telling on the way here really true?" asked Kara.

"Of course they were. Do you think we would make up stories just to keep the adventure interesting?" Mandy answered with a twinkle in her eye.

"I've heard those stories since I came here, so I know they're true," Alex added.

"Right," Riley said, not believing either of them.

"We'll hang here for a bit and let people wade and swim before we get into the kayaks," said Mandy.

"That should be fun," said Riley.

"I'll give everyone a tour around the island and tell you a little about the ecosystem and history."

"I had no idea these tours were so educational," said Kara.

"We're proud of our heritage and try to maintain and preserve our treasures," explained Mandy. "Isn't that right, Alex?"

"It sure is. Most of the natives want tourists to get to know our islands and treasure it the way we do," said Alex. "Let's go wade a little," she added, getting up and taking Riley with her.

It wasn't long until the kayaks were unloaded, and everyone that wanted to grabbed a boat with a partner and followed Mandy around the island for the ecosystem tour. Kara was particularly happy because she was in the boat with Mandy.

After that, they lounged and played on the beach until it was time to board the boat and sail back to where they started. The trip back was quiet and peaceful. Riley sat between Alex's legs and leaned back, enjoying the ride. What a perfect end to this first adventure.

When they got back, Kara decided to wait until Mandy was finished unloading the boat, so Riley and Alex left to go to Alex's apartment. She told Kara that she wasn't going back to the hotel that night and the room was hers.

Alex and Riley strolled into Peaches hand in hand to

find Liz at the bar and Beverly and Max taking care of the few patrons.

"Well, you two look like you just came in from the sea," Liz said.

"We did, and what fun it was," Riley told Liz. She went on to tell Liz what all they did for the day and what all she saw snorkeling.

When she stopped, Liz looked at both Alex and Riley but didn't say anything.

"What?" Alex asked.

"You two look so happy," Liz explained. "Before you say anything, Alex, I'm not teasing you like I usually do. You look happy, and so does Riley. This day agreed with both of you."

Alex looked at Riley and smiled. "It's okay, Liz. I know I give you a hard time because you *are* always teasing me, but you're right. We had a great time today, and I know I look happy because I am."

"Do you usually not look happy?" Riley asked. "Because you're always happy with me."

"That should tell you something right there!" Liz answered for them all.

Alex said, "Well, I'm not an unhappy person, but you're right, Riley. I am always happy with you." She felt herself waver then, as though she might spill all of her secrets right there in public, so she took a minute to compose herself and change the subject. "And what would make me happy right now is food! Adventuring and happiness make me hungry!"

Everyone laughed, and Riley agreed. "Let's go back to my place, get my stuff, and find us some food."

"Are you feeling fancy or not?" Liz asked.

"Not. I'm too tired to make myself presentable after today," Riley said looking at Alex hoping she'd agree.

"Let's get your stuff, hit the food trucks, and go upstairs for a rooftop feast," Alex offered.

"Perfect!" Riley said, grabbing Alex's hand and pulling her toward the door.

"See y'all later!" Alex said as they left.

Liz smiled to herself

"What's that look for?" asked Beverly.

"Oh, my little Alex is falling in love. Isn't it beautiful?" Liz said happily.

"It's about time," Beverly said.

"It sure is. Now if we can just keep her from messing this up."

"Fingers crossed."

* * *

"That was just right," Riley said wiping her hands on her napkin. "I love fish tacos."

"Me too. Would you like another beer?" Alex offered.

"I think I've had my fill for the day," said Riley, stretching. "What I'd really like is to cuddle up with you on that couch and watch these beautiful stars come out."

"That can be arranged. Let me throw this in the trash so it won't blow away."

Alex finished tidying up and then pulled Riley over to one of the chaise lounges. "Let's sit here. We can put our feet up, and it'll be more comfortable." She wrapped her arm around Riley's shoulder. Riley took a deep breath and laid her head on Alex's shoulder.

"It's kind of hard to see stars from there, isn't it?" asked Alex.

"Maybe, but it's also so comfortable. I think your shoulder was made just for me."

"Really?"

"Can't you feel how perfectly I fit right here?" Riley said. She began kissing Alex's neck.

"Mm, I sure do," Alex moaned.

"I swear I was so tired I wanted to lay my head down a minute, and then my lips took over and they can't seem to stop," Riley said as she kissed her way up to Alex's ear and tugged on the lobe.

"I love your lips. I don't ever want them to stop."

Riley leaned up and kissed Alex, slowly at first and then she brought the heat. Alex pulled the bottom of Riley's shirt up, lifting it over her head.

"We have too many clothes on," Riley said, sitting up and taking her bra and shorts off. She looked at Alex with a 'what are you waiting for' look. Alex jumped up and out of her clothes. Riley pushed her back down and straddled her hips.

"I missed you last night," Riley said, "and I intend to show you how much." Her lips crashed into Alex's. They both moaned when Riley's breasts pressed into Alex. Alex's hands flew to Riley's back, pulling her closer. Riley kissed her way down Alex's chest to her nipples, lavishing each like she'd never touched them before.

Riley then sat up so Alex's mouth landed right where she needed it, moving from one nipple to the other. Riley scooted down a little so she could get her hand between them. Alex did the same. They locked into one another's eyes as they slowly guided fingers inside each other. Riley gasped and began to ride Alex slowly while keeping two fingers inside her. They found their rhythm, one with the other, never losing eye contact. Their breathing began to quicken, but their pace was steady. Neither wanted to rush how good this building fire inside of them felt. The fire began to explode, and Riley stiffened right before Alex did the same. She willed Alex to see inside her heart at what was growing but, she was afraid to say the words and then she collapsed on Alex's chest.

After a few moments catching their breaths, they came back to themselves.

"That was incredible," Alex whispered breathlessly.

"Intense!" Riley said into Alex's chest. Then she raised up and kissed Alex softly, not wanting their connection to end.

6

The days flew by, full of laughter, adventure, food, friendship, and fun. Some days Alex was able to spend all day with Riley. Kara joined them when she was not networking with contacts, and Mandy was included when she wasn't working. On days when Alex worked, Riley explored on her own, taking tons of pictures to the point that she thought about starting a blog. She fell more in love with the islands each day she was there.

She tried not to think about her vacation coming to an end. That would mean leaving Alex. Kara kept reminding her that there was no reason she had to go home right away. After all, she was retired now. This thought was in the back of her mind, but she wasn't sure what Alex would think if she announced that she was staying. They both suspected this was more than a vacation fling, maybe it was time that she found a little courage and asked Alex how she would feel about her staying longer.

Riley walked into Peaches with only a few days left on her vacation to find it busy. Her talk with Alex would have to wait. She walked over to the bar as Alex and Liz mixed drinks and filled orders as quickly as they could. Alex smiled at her but kept mixing.

"What can I do to help? This is the place to be tonight!" Riley said.

"Some nights are like this," Alex answered.

"Hand me a tray and a rag. I can at least clear tables until you get caught up," offered Riley.

"You don't have to do that," said Alex.

"I know, but I want to," Riley said reaching for the tray Liz handed her.

A couple of hours later Riley sat down at the bar to catch her breath. "Wow, I've never seen it this busy. Did a cruise ship come in or something?"

Alex laughed. "No, a couple of big groups hit at the same time along with the regulars. Thanks for helping out. You really didn't have to do that."

"But we sure do appreciate it!" Liz added. "We haven't been slammed like that in quite some time. Maybe you have a future as a barmaid, Riley."

Riley laughed. "Nothing like on-the-job training!"

Alex came around from behind the bar with two beers, stuck out her arm for Riley to take, and led her onto the patio. She handed Riley a beer and said, "Now that it has quieted down, tell me how your day was."

"Not bad, especially for the last couple of hours," Riley said smiling and taking a long drink.

Alex leaned over and gave her a quick kiss on the lips. "I've wanted to do that when you walked in."

"Do you have a busy day tomorrow? I was hoping we could spend a little time together," Riley said.

"Actually, I'm hoping I have a date tomorrow with this hot little redhead. Why? What did you have in mind?"

Riley laughed. "Hot little redhead, huh? Well, it'd better

be this little redhead because I plan on spending every minute with you!"

Alex smiled. "I hoped we could ride bikes over to the national park and have a picnic. I've wanted to show you the park since you've been here, but we haven't been able to work it in."

"I'd love that!" Riley enthused. "I miss riding my bike."

"Then it's a date."

"I have tons of pictures to show you that I took today. I find something new every day that amazes me."

"Well, I'll be here for a while longer."

"I know, I don't mind. I thought I'd just hang around until you were finished."

"Hmm, would you want to spend the night?"

"I thought you'd never ask," Riley said with a chuckle.

The bar continued to be busy, so Riley helped out until they closed. They both made it up to Alex's around two in the morning and fell into bed exhausted. "I can't wait to show you the places I love by bike tomorrow," Alex said yawning.

"I can't wait to see them," Riley said sleepily. She gathered Alex into her arms, kissed her on the forehead, and in minutes they were both fast asleep.

Alex dreamed that she and Riley were at one of her favorite spots on the island. She was telling Riley about what led her to the island. After telling Riley the whole story, she took Alex in her arms and told her everything was going to be alright. Alex woke up with a smile on her face, then realized it was just a dream. She looked over at Riley, her face so peaceful. Maybe she would tell her today. She was going to do it anyway, so why not today? It was a risk, but she'd already risked so much with Riley. She was falling in love with her—wasn't that the biggest risk of all? Alex thought so, and it had happened when she wasn't looking. She kissed Riley's forehead and snuggled next to her and went back to sleep.

The next morning they prepared for their ride. Alex left Riley upstairs packing them a picnic while she went downstairs to get drinks for the ride. Liz was there doing inventory for a liquor order when Alex said, "Good morning."

"Hey there, getting ready to go?"

"Yes, I needed to get a few drinks together to take with us. I'm so excited about this ride."

"I can tell," Liz said, smiling.

"I've decided I'm going to tell Riley about Texas and what happened," said Alex.

"Good for you! I'm so glad. What made you decide to do that?" Liz asked.

"You're right. I've got to take a chance on Riley. I trust her and don't want to keep secrets from her. I also don't want what we have to end, so I'm really scared."

"I know you're scared, but Alex, Riley is a good person. We know that. She'll understand, just like I do," Liz said putting an arm around Alex's shoulder and squeezing.

"God, I hope so."

Riley walked in just then, the picnic bag slung over her shoulder. "You hope what?"

"I hoped you were ready to go!" Alex said, looking at Liz and then Riley.

"You two have a good time. Don't let her wear you out, Riley," said Liz.

"Do you mean the bike or..." Riley said, watching as Alex's cheeks reddened. They all laughed.

"Get out of here," Liz said pushing them to the door.

They loaded up the bikes and headed to the national park. It was a beautiful day with little wind and plenty of sunshine. They took their time, with Riley taking everything in and asking question after question about the monuments, landscape, and more. Several people honked or waved to Alex, and she would explain who they were.

Riley asked to stop and take a few pictures when a truck came speeding past and a man yelled, "Get out of the way you pervert!"

Riley jumped back and said, "What the hell was that?"

Alex pretended she didn't know who it was and said, "Obviously some ass hole." She recognized the truck as a convenience store owner that had suspicions about her.

Thankfully Riley let it go as they made it to the park, Alex pointed out a couple of trails that they could hike another day. She led them down one that opened up to a secluded cove. They were the only ones on the beach. Together they parked the bikes and unloaded their backpacks. Riley spread a blanket out on the sand, and Alex placed the food and drinks nearby.

"Let's wade in the water and cool off a little," said Alex.

They played in the water, splashing around, and Riley jumped on Alex's back with her arms around her neck. Alex grabbed her legs and held her there. "You make me feel like a kid!" Riley yelled, squeezing Alex.

"A kid?" Alex said as she walked farther into the water.

"Alex, what are you doing? Alex, wait, oh no. Babe, don't let me go!"

"I can't seem to hold on," Alex said, dumping Riley into the water.

Riley came up just as Alex turned, and she pulled Alex under the water with her. They both came up, laughing, arms around each other.

"Babe, huh?" Alex said, her eyebrows raised.

"Yeah. Babe. You have a problem with that?"

Alex smiled, then kissed Riley hard, holding her as tight as possible.

"Mm, I'm calling you babe all the time if you kiss me like that!" Riley said.

They made their way out of the water and back to the food and drinks. When they finished their meal, they lay back on the blanket and watched the clouds, holding hands. "This has been the best date ever," Riley said, squeezing Alex's hand.

"It's not over yet."

Riley sat up and looked down at Alex. "I need to talk to you about something," she said hesitantly.

Alex froze, maybe today wasn't the day to talk to Riley after all. "Okay?"

Riley had Alex's hand in both of hers, trying to find courage. "What would you think if I didn't have to leave at the end of the week?"

"I think that would be like a Christmas gift in July!" Alex said, sitting up.

"Really?" Riley said.

Alex nodded as her heart sped up.

"Well, you know I'm not teaching anymore and I don't have anything that I have to be home for this summer," she explained.

"And that means?"

"That means I could stay here for a while."

"Really! That would be wonderful! Do you want to stay?"

"I do." Riley's eyes sparkled as they took in her surroundings. "I'm finding that I love this place more and more every day. I feel so relaxed here, and there's something new every day. I love taking pictures, and I'm thinking about starting a blog or a book. I even love working at the bar!"

Riley said, not quite admitting why she really wanted to stay.

Alex looked at her, beaming.

"I wish you'd say something," Riley said, a little uneasy despite Alex's grin.

"I'm having a hard time expressing how happy that would make me, you staying."

Riley smiled and put her arms around Alex's neck. "I'm not trying to pressure us," she said quietly. "But I don't want to go home, I want to stay here in this beautiful paradise. I want to stay here with you." She looked into Alex's eyes longingly.

"Oh, Riley, I want you to stay here with me. And I don't mean in your hotel or somewhere else. I want you to stay with me," Alex said.

"You're not worried about what people are going to say? About how fast we're moving, I mean."

"I quit worrying about what people think a long time ago, Riley. I'm certainly not going to let them mess this up with their unwanted opinions," Alex said taking Riley's face in her hands. "I'm in love with you, Riley." Alex couldn't believe she actually said this out loud, but there was no going back and she didn't want to. She was in love with Riley James and didn't care who knew.

"Oh Alex, I'm in love with you too," Riley said, kissing Alex long and slow.

When they parted Alex asked Riley, "Do you believe in love at first sight?"

Riley chuckled. "I do now!" They both laughed.

"The day that you and your friends walked into the bar was a strange day for me. I had a feeling that something was coming. I get those sometimes, if you know what I mean?"

Riley nodded, letting Alex continue.

"It bothered me all day, and I tried to put it aside when you walked into the bar. I couldn't keep my eyes off of you as you now know, but as the evening went on and you ended up spending the night with me I didn't think about it again until I was walking back to my place after leaving you at the dock the next morning. I noticed the feeling had been replaced by a... this is hard to explain. But it was replaced by a fullness and peacefulness that I'd never felt before." Alex paused to take a deep breath and continued.

"I knew it was because of you. I didn't want to admit that at first because it was scary," she said, looking down and tracing the sand with her fingers. "But I haven't let anyone close to me in a very long time, Riley. And I know now that I couldn't stop this even if I tried."

"I know what you mean," Riley said. "Alex, no one has ever looked at me the way you do. Sometimes I lose myself in your eyes and the world stops. But do you remember that night on the beach when Liz told us to go watch the sun set?"

"Of course I remember," Alex said. "That kiss."

"That kiss," Riley said, whispering close to Alex's lips. "It felt like my heart leapt right out of my chest into yours. It was the best feeling, but it scared me to death." She looked straight into Alex's eyes and said with a clear, strong voice, "I'm not scared anymore."

At that moment Alex knew this was not the time to tell Riley about her past. Relieved, the time for talking was over, Alex's mouth crushed Riley's as she pushed her down on the blanket. Her hand reached under Riley's shirt and cupped her breast through her swimsuit top. Riley moaned and reached down and shimmied out of her swim suit bottoms. Their lips only parted for Alex to settle between Riley's legs. Her hand slid down Riley's stomach and cupped her sex.

"Oh god, Alex," Riley breathed.

Alex separated Riley's lips and was greeted by wetness as she slid through her folds. Riley's hips bucked into Alex's hand. She took her finger and stroked Riley from her entrance, up and around her swollen bud. She did this over and over as Riley writhed under her.

"Shit—Alex, please. Take me, make me yours," she pleaded.

Alex didn't need any urging. She entered Riley slowly, then added another finger. Riley's breath hitched, and she moaned, "God, that's good."

She went to work, stroking in and out slowly, then quickened her pace as Riley's arms tightened around her. Alex kissed her, swallowing Riley's screams of pleasure. Her fingers stayed inside and curled upward as Riley's orgasm took her in waves. They stayed like this for several moments and then Riley's arms fell to the blanket completely spent.

Alex whispered into Riley's ear, "You're mine."

"I am." Riley smiled, trying to catch her breath. "Now what are you going to do with me?"

Alex lay down next to her and said playfully, "Hmm, that's a very good question."

Riley raised up on her elbow, putting her head in her hand. "It's a little late for this question since my naked backside is shining for anyone to see, but is there a possibility someone could see us?"

"I guess there's always a possibility, but I've never seen anyone else and I come here every week."

"Good to know. Because if someone comes up now they're about to get quite a show," Riley said. She reached down and took Alex's swimsuit bottoms off. "I intend to make you mine here and now." She leaned down and kissed Alex possessively. A light breeze rustled the trees, the water lapped gently to the shore, and Riley thought this was the best moment of her life.

* * *

Riley and Alex spent the afternoon lazing on the blanket and swimming in the cove. No one came down the trail, and it truly felt like their own secluded beach. They were ravenous from lovemaking and swimming and ate the rest of their picnic. After one last swim they lay down on the blanket to let the sun dry them and get ready for the bike ride back to town.

They were lying there holding hands when Alex said, "This has been the best day."

"Mm, it sure has."

"I would like to ask you for a favor," said Alex.

"Anything, babe."

Alex smiled at the term of endearment. "A lot has happened today. I know we still have a lot to talk about, but could we soak this up for a while? We don't have to try and cram everything into a few days like before. We have time now." She looked over at Riley and pulled her hand to her mouth, kissing the back of it. "I don't know what movies you like or what kind of books you like to read? I don't even know your favorite color!"

Riley said chuckling, "Is it strange we haven't talked about all of this? I mean does it matter?"

"I don't think it's strange because we've been trying to do so many things before you left that had nothing to do with movies, books and the like. But I want to know everything about you."

"Okay then, I like most movies, but I'm not too keen on horror. Let's see, books. I'm into lesfic, and I'll admit I'm a sucker for a lesbian romance, but I do read bestsellers, too. My favorite color is blue, more like a greenish blue, like the color of the beautiful water from your rooftop deck when afternoon begins to turn into evening. How's that? Now it's your turn."

"Lesbian romance?" Alex giggled. "I feel like I'm living a lesbian romance!" *I so hope it has a happily-ever-after ending,* she thought to herself.

"Come on, movies, music, and books. Now go," Riley said.

"Okay. I like all movies including horror. I'll hold you close so you don't have to be scared when we watch them. I don't listen to much country, but I'm a sap for a good love song. I read mysteries and thrillers and love a good detective story. I try to figure it out before the hero does. I have recently found a new favorite color."

Riley looked at her questioningly. "You have?"

"It would be green that sometimes changes to hazel or turns a little blue."

"Where did you see that?"

"I'm looking right at it," Alex said, drinking in Riley's eyes. "It's a sparkling shade of green."

Riley blushed. "Oh my god, you are such a charmer."

"Evidently you bring it out in me."

Riley rolled closer to Alex and pecked her lips.

"Let's go back to Peaches and celebrate our newfound courage and love," Alex said.

"That's a great idea. I'll call Kara and tell her to bring Mandy along."

"I'll make Liz sneak away long enough for dinner, and we'll share our good news with them."

"Sounds like a plan. I think I have enough energy left to ride back to town."

"You'd better, darlin'. We have celebrating to do!" She gave Riley a kiss on the lips before jumping up. They put their clothes on, cleaned up the area, and packed what was left of their picnic.

Before getting on the bikes, Riley took Alex in her arms and said, "I'm going to remember this day for the rest of my life. This is our place. Okay?"

"Our place," Alex said, testing it on her tongue. "I love it, and I love you." She pulled Riley close and kissed her tenderly.

"Stop doing that or we'll never leave," Riley said.

She let Alex go, winked at her, and got on her bike. The ride back was full of more questions from Riley and more beautiful vistas at every turn. Alex loved answering her questions, pointing out boats on the water, and explaining parts of the park. She wanted to share all of the islands with Riley and show her why they were important to her and why she loved them.

There was a hint of foreboding coming in and out of Alex's mind. Despite how much they'd discussed, how far their relationship was going, she still hadn't told Riley why she stayed here and didn't go back to the States. There was also relief because now she had time. She would find the right moment to tell Riley the whole story. Then they could talk about the future. Alex so hoped they had a future. She looked over at Riley, her hair blowing in the breeze, her happy face smiling, pedaling away. About that time Riley looked over and blew Alex a kiss. That story would have to wait, she decided. It was the furthest thing from her mind now.

When they made it back to Alex's, Riley called Kara and Alex talked with Liz. They all agreed to meet on the patio of Peaches in an hour. While Alex was in the shower, Riley wandered up to the roof. This had quickly turned into one of her favorite places. She looked out at the boats bobbing in the beautiful blue water. Alex loved her. She had said it, and Riley said it right back. To say they were both surprised would be true. Riley had been thinking this but afraid to say it out loud. Now that she had, what would happen next?

She had a lot to contemplate. This was big. Her whole life was back in Florida, but there was no Alex in Florida. Maybe she should try this love on for a while, let it soak all the way through her. It might be new, but in some ways it felt comfortable like an old, soft T-shirt. She'd always been a romantic at heart, and this had been some kind of whirlwind. Now that she'd told Alex she loved her, she felt like the whirlwind had set her down right where she was meant to be. She felt arms softly close around her from behind. She leaned back and smiled.

"You're a million miles away," Alex said softly.

"No, I'm not. I'm right here, letting all this sink in. I feel like I'm living again. My life before had become mundane. And now, I haven't only fallen in love, I'm living this love," she said turning in Alex's arms. "When I came on this trip I had no idea what I was going to do with my life, but now, there's you."

Alex stared into Riley's eyes and softly said, "Live this love, that's us, isn't it?"

Riley laughed and threw her head back, "I love Alex Adams, and I'm telling the world!"

"Whoa," it was Alex's turn to laugh. "Slow down, it's just our little world."

"And I love our little world. We'd better get down there to welcome our guests since we invited them," she said giving Alex a quick kiss.

They headed to the patio through the bar and noticed it

wasn't crowded at all. Liz would be able to join them without worrying. Alex couldn't help but wonder what everyone would think about Riley's decision to stay.

She had told Riley that she had stopped worrying about what everyone would think, but this was still moving so fast. However, to Alex it seemed like she'd been waiting all these years to feel like this, not to be scared of her past but to look forward to a future. When she really thought about it, she realized that after settling on the island and at the bar her life was simply work. For all those years she never dreamed that someone would want to share her life with her, that someone would care when she came home or want to ride bikes or hear what she thought until Riley James walked into Peaches

7

"Hey, lovebirds," Kara said with a twinkle in her eye. "Mandy will be here shortly, she's finishing up on the boat."

"Hey, yourself," Riley said.

"What can I get you ladies to drink? I'm heading for the bar," Alex asked.

"Beer for me, babe."

Kara chuckled and said playfully, "I'll take a beer, too, babe."

Alex shook her head and walked off smiling.

"So how was the big date today?"

Riley sighed. "It was perfect, Kara."

"Oh yeah?"

"Yeah, we had the best day. Alex has a little secluded place with its own cove. It felt like we were on our own private island. We didn't see or hear another person the entire time."

"Uh-huh, so what in the world did you two find to do?"

"Well, we..." Riley's cheeks began to redden, but she

didn't finish her sentence as Alex walked in with their beers along with Liz and Mandy.

"Hi, everybody!"

"How nice of you two to have us all over for dinner," Liz said. "But I have an idea there's a little more to this, so spill."

"Have a seat, what makes you think there's more to a group of friends finding time to share a meal together?" said Alex.

"Share a meal together, when have you ever said that in your life?" Liz teased.

"I just did," Alex said laughing.

"Come on, I'm with Liz. What's going on, lovebirds?" Kara said.

"Lovebirds! Do you have to keep calling us that, Kara?" Riley asked.

"If the flip flop fits," she replied. Everybody laughed.

"Actually, I do have something to share with you all," Riley confessed, feeling nervous as she looked to Alex for support. Alex grabbed her hand under the table and gave it a little squeeze for encouragement.

"I've decided to stay on the island," she announced.

"Stay? That's awesome!" exclaimed Liz.

"For how long?" asked Kara.

"I'm not really sure because I just made up my mind and told Alex today," she said smiling at Alex. "Actually, you gave me the idea, Kara."

"I did?"

"Yes, you know exactly what I'm talking about. You said, 'You know, Riley, you don't have anything you have to be home to do.'"

"Of course I remember saying that. I just didn't think you listened to me," she said with a laugh.

"I listened and thought it over and realized you're right.

There's nothing I can't do from here, so why not stay in paradise?"

"It is paradise, but I don't think that's why you're staying," Kara teased. "What about clothes?"

"Clothes? She doesn't need clothes," Liz said. Kara and Mandy laughed as Riley and Alex both turned red.

"Oh, come on, get your minds out of the gutter. She doesn't need clothes because all you wear here are shorts, T-shirts, and swim suits," Liz said.

Everyone joined in laughing, and Mandy said, "That's great, Riley. It'll be nice having you here. I've never seen Alex smile so much." She turned to Alex. "I've known you since I was a kid, and you really look happy."

"You're right," Alex said, "I don't know when I've been this happy."

"Okay, so we're all happy you're staying. Let's celebrate! I'm hungry!" said Liz.

They ate, drank, and shared stories until it was time for Peaches to close. As Alex and Mandy cleared the table Riley pulled Kara aside.

"I want to stay with Alex tonight if you don't mind."

"No problem, I have plans with Mandy anyway. But we'll talk tomorrow because I don't think you're telling me everything," Kara said, hugging Riley.

"I'll see you in the morning."

"Deal. Mandy, we have the place to ourselves tonight. Let's go," Kara said grabbing Mandy's hand. Mandy blushed but said goodbye to everyone.

"Welcome, Riley. I'm so glad you'll be staying on with us," Liz said pulling her into a hug. To Alex she winked and said, "I'll see you in the morning, not early."

"See you in the morning," Alex said putting her arm

around Riley. "That went well. Everyone is really glad you're staying, but..."

"But what?" Riley said nervously.

"But I'm the happiest of all. This may be the best summer ever," Alex said holding Riley tight.

* * *

Riley walked to the hotel in such a happy mood. The heady scent of tropical flowers wafted on the light cool breeze. People on the street smiled at her as she nodded or returned their hellos. She didn't think anything could take the smile off her face. When she got to Kara's door, she knocked.

"Why are you knocking? This is your room, too," Kara said as she answered the door.

"I didn't want to interrupt anything."

"Ha, ha. Mandy and I have fun together, but we're not lovebirds like you and Alex."

"Very funny. Speaking of love..." Riley hinted.

"Yes?" Kara said, dragging the word out.

"Yesterday while we were at the park, I was telling Alex that I wanted to stay here. She said if I stayed it would be like having Christmas in July."

"Uh-huh? Come on, Riley. You're killing me here."

"She said she was in love with me and wants me to move in with her!" Riley said, the words spilling out.

Kara hugged her. "That's great. What did you say?"

"I told her I'm in love with her, too. I know this is fast, Kara, but before you give me a lecture," Riley said.

Kara held her hand up. "I'm not going to give you a lecture. I think it's great! It's just a little strange because you're the one that plans everything out and is so responsible and I'm usually the one jumping right in."

"I know, but when I was trying to think all of this through, I couldn't come up with one reason to go home. I realized that I've just been going through the motions, not really living. When I'm with Alex, we have fun and I'm so happy. I can't tell you what a difference it made when I told her I was staying. It was like we didn't have to cram everything into two weeks. Now we have time to get to know one another better and not have to hurry and worry about me leaving and what we're going to do."

"What about your family? They should be all right with this, right?"

"Yeah, Mom and Dad are off traveling again. My brothers have their own lives. The kids don't really need their Aunt Riley anymore."

Kara folded her arms. "I know that's not true. You're their Super Aunt."

"I am, but they're busy with college and friends, and really the only time I see them anymore is at the holidays."

"Imagine how fun it will be when they come visit!"

"Come visit?" Riley asked.

"Sure. You're not going to be running back and forth between here and Florida. Maybe they can come here for the holidays."

"Kara, you sound like I'm staying permanently."

"Why not? Do you really think it's going to be any easier leaving Alex in two months? Because she's not going anywhere. She has a business here."

"Yeah, but I have a house and a life back in Florida."

"You just said you were going through the motions, and it's just a house, Riley. You can sell a house."

"I know, but this is already moving so fast and I don't want to get that far ahead of myself. Besides, what if Alex doesn't feel the same way? You're talking about me moving here, Alex and me making a life together."

"Believe me, she feels the same way," Kara said. "Mandy has told me about Alex. She never dates. Her family comes to visit, but she's never seen her with another woman."

"I know. That does seem a little odd because I'm telling you she's wonderful. But then again you don't see me with anybody either."

"Maybe she's scared of commitment."

"I don't know, I don't think that's it. But there is something," Riley said. "She told me once that she'd tell me the whole story on how she got here and why she stayed. I mean she told me that she and her friend came here for vacation and that she decided to stay after meeting Liz."

"Yeah, Mandy said that there's something back where Alex came from that made her stay here. She said that's what people say, but no one knows for sure. They're just stories."

"We haven't talked about her past much. I know she was a financial advisor in Dallas but didn't like her job when she came here, so that's why she took the chance and stayed. As the years went by, she became Liz's partner. When she talks about it there's a sadness in her eyes that's not there otherwise. There's something she's not telling me, but I'm sure with time she will."

"I don't think it could be that bad. Everyone here loves her, and she's partners with Liz, who seems like a person to trust. How bad could it be?"

"I don't know. I hope she realizes she can trust me and tell me anything." She smiled. "That's why I'm staying. We're going to get to know one another better and see what we have here."

"So, what are you going to do while she's working? Soak up the sun, walk the beach, be a bum?"

"No way. When I left school this year, I decided I was going to find something else to do. I have helped at the bar and loved it, so I'm going to tell Alex I'll fill in when needed. Surely, I can find something to do."

"You will." Kara's eyes popped open as she got an idea. "Why don't you write that book you've always wanted to. You have the talent, and you've never failed at anything you set out to do."

"Actually, I've been thinking about that. This would be the perfect time to see if I have an author living inside me. What I want to know is how am I going to get by without my best friend right around the corner."

"You have a phone; we'll be fine. Besides, I'm planning to come back. I've made a few connections that would be a perfect reason to come visit."

"That makes me feel better," Riley said, hugging Kara.

* * *

Alex was stocking the bar and doing other chores to get ready to open. She thought about how nice it was last night after their little celebration to relax. It had been a big day filled with changes—good changes, full of hope. It seemed like she and Riley were always in a hurry to get everything in before Riley had to leave. Now they could relax a bit and soak up one another without a deadline looming. She thought again how happy this summer was going to be. Sometimes she wanted to pinch herself to make sure this was real. Riley James loved her and was staying here with her. A big smile was on her face when Liz walked in. She looked around like she was expecting someone.

"What or who are you looking for?" Alex asked.

"I'm looking for that beautiful girlfriend of yours. She has to be around here someplace for you to have that big smile plastered on your face."

"Girlfriend. I like the sound of that," said Alex.

"Where is she?"

"She went to help Kara pack up. Her flight leaves tomorrow. I'm so happy Riley will not be getting on that plane."

"I know you are, honey."

"Liz, she told me she's in love with me."

"She did! And what did you say?"

"Actually, I told her first. She told me she was staying, and I was so happy. I asked her to live here with me. I just blurted it out. The words were out of my mouth before I knew what I was saying. Then, I told her I was in love with her. I couldn't believe I said it."

Liz was smiling as she asked, "Are you sorry you said it?"

"No! I don't know what's come over me, Liz. I've never felt like this about anyone, and it's so wonderful. It's the best feeling ever; Riley is amazing. So, what in the world is she doing with me? I can't believe it!" said Alex, shaking her head.

"What do you mean? You happen to be amazing, too! You are both lucky to have found one another. Or maybe it was fate."

Alex raised a skeptical eyebrow. "Fate?"

"We know you're not with anyone because you don't think you deserve it, which is entirely wrong. But Riley isn't with anyone either, and you two just happen to meet? The stars are in your favor, sweetheart."

"I hope they stay that way."

"It's up to you two now. She loves you, you love her, now build a life."

Alex quieted at that and dropped her head. "I haven't told her, Liz."

Liz walked over and stood in front of Alex. She tilted Alex's chin up with her hand and said, "I see. Why haven't you told her? She deserves to know, Alex."

"I know she does. I took her to the park and planned to explain it all to her. Before I could, she grabbed my hands and told me she was staying. All I could feel when she said that was happiness. The past left my body like it had never happened. The next thing I knew I told her I was in love with her and she said it back. I cannot tell you how that felt, Liz. It's like my fucked-up heart had been healed, and I was a whole person again. How in the hell am I supposed to tell her after that?" Alex said with tears in her eyes.

Liz wrapped her arms around Alex and held her close. "My sweet Alex. It will be okay, you have to trust Riley." She loosened her hold and put her hands on Alex's shoulders, looking her in the eyes, "You can't expect to build a life with Riley if you can't share your life with her."

Alex nodded. "I know you're right, but I think I'm more scared than ever now."

"You had the courage to tell her you love her, and you'll find the courage to tell her your story. You can work through this and find the words. I wish I could do it for you, but you have to do this for yourself and for Riley."

Alex took a deep breath. "I will, Liz. I'll find a way."

"Good girl. You know I'm always here for you."

"I do, and I'm thankful every day."

* * *

June flew by and they found themselves in late July before they knew it; the bar was busy with vacationers, and Riley helped when needed. She and Alex had settled into a nice rhythm. In the mornings they biked or went for a run. One of their favorite things to do was paddle-boarding. Alex worked most nights, but Riley was always waiting when she came home. Whenever they had a lazy morning, they would have coffee on the rooftop deck and imagine where the boats in the harbor were going or coming from.

Riley found that she loved writing. She had dabbled in it from time to time in the past, but with more time she was able to hone her ability and use it for a job. Through Kara's connections she found clients and wrote product descriptions or content for websites and could do it all online. She also was outlining the book she hoped to write. When she wasn't writing her days were filled with exploring the surrounding community. The locals made her feel welcome, well, most of them. There were a few people, when they found out she lived with Alex, walked away. It was odd, she mentioned it to Liz once and she shrugged it off.

Riley had talked to her parents and told them she was staying and why. They were a little concerned because this was out of character for Riley, but she assured them that she was with good people in a good place and most of all that she was happy. Her brothers weren't so sure, but their kids thought it was cool. As time passed and they met Alex through video visits, their reservations softened.

Alex told her sister all about Riley. This was the first time she had told her about anyone besides Liz and her coworkers. Her family was so happy she had found someone to spend time with other than the people at work. Her sister, Samantha, niece, Rosie, and her daughter, Sasha, were due for a visit and couldn't wait to meet this woman that Alex was so smitten with.

Riley was just about finished with her morning writing

session when her phone rang. She looked at the screen and saw it was Kara.

"Hey stranger, I thought you'd forgotten all about me," Riley said answering.

"Not possible. I've been so freaking busy lately but, I've gotten your texts. What's happening in paradise?"

"The sun is shining and I'm writing. Alex is at work."

"How are you and Alex? Still love birds?"

"Of course. Her sister and her family are coming for a visit soon and I'm getting a little nervous."

"They'll love you."

"I hope so."

"Listen Ri, Sara called me today being rather mysterious."

Riley felt her stomach fall and said, "Mysterious?"

"Yeah, she asked how you and Alex were doing. Then she said there was something in Alex's past that you should be aware of. Has she told you anything?"

"No, nothing bad. What did she say it was?"

"That's just it, she didn't. She was going to call you but, saw how happy you both looked on social media and decided to call me instead."

"We are happy. Did she say how she got the information?"

"No, she didn't. But, let me ask you this, do you trust Alex?"

"Of course I do."

"You know maybe she hasn't told you because it's in the past and you are her future."

"She's my future too. When I retired, I didn't have any idea what would happen and it was scary. But with Alex, I have a purpose, every day is an adventure."

"Maybe it hasn't been the right time. Think about it,

you've only been there a couple of months. I think you should wait her out."

"I know there's something because she gets this sadness in her eyes. I haven't pushed her because I thought she'd tell me eventually. What could it be?"

"I don't know, maybe you should ask her?"

"Ask her what? It's funny Sara wouldn't tell you what it was."

"It is ... but, bottom line, you trust Alex."

"I do Kara. Maybe she'll tell me when her family gets here."

"Makes sense, if it's her past her family would be involved."

"Shit, I hate this."

"Me too. You know, it can't be anything too terrible because Liz and Mandy love her and so do the people on the island."

Riley suddenly remembered the man that yelled at them on the bikes. "If she doesn't tell me while her family is here, I'll ask but, not before then. I don't want to mess up this visit."

"That sounds good. You know her a lot better than me, but Riley, if you trust her so do I."

"Thanks. I'll let you know what happens."

"I love you, Riley."

"Love you too." Riley ended the call and felt very unsettled. Alex is a good person, she knew that, she trusted her, but something told her this might be a test of their relationship.

* * *

One morning after swimming and paddling together they made their way back to Alex's so she could get ready for work. "That was so much fun. You're getting better and better on that paddleboard, babe," Alex said.

"Thanks. I'll admit I've been going some when you have to work in the afternoons."

"Oh, so that's how you are, sneaking around on me," Alex said grabbing Riley playfully around the waist.

"I wasn't exactly sneaking. If you look out the patio, you could see me."

"Oh, I saw you all right. The hottest babe on the beach."

Riley laughed. "Hardly, but thanks for saying that, baby. I know you get off early tonight, so I want to take you on a date. We've been so busy lately, and you're so tired when you get in from work I thought it'd be nice."

"A date? There's no one else I'd rather go out with. I accept," Alex said smiling.

"Well, we don't really have to go out. I thought I'd cook, and we'd have dinner on the roof. We haven't done that in ages."

"That sounds even better. I can't wait," Alex said, giving Riley a quick kiss. "I've got to get in the shower so I can get to work and come back to you."

Riley laughed. "You'd better hurry then."

It had been a few days since her conversation with Kara. She played it over and over but still, she always came back to her trust in Alex. It was becoming harder not to say anything but, she was staying with her plan of waiting until after her family had been here. The day passed quickly, and Riley almost had everything ready for dinner when Alex came home.

"Wow, something smells delicious," Alex said, coming into the kitchen area. Riley came out of the bedroom in a strappy dress that fell just above her knees. She had styled her hair and was wearing makeup.

"Get away from there. It's not quite done," Riley said walking toward Alex.

"Oh wow! Riley, you look beautiful," Alex said softly. "Stay away, I smell terrible. Someone spilled beer all over me."

"I will not stay away," Riley said taking Alex's face in her hands and kissing her softly. "I missed you today. You have time to shower before dinner is ready."

"I'll be fast," Alex said walking to the bathroom. She stopped and turned looking at Riley. "You are the most beautiful woman."

Riley smiled and winked. "Thank you. When you're finished, meet me on the roof."

While Alex was showering, Riley set everything up on the roof. It was a simple supper of grilled shrimp, pilaf, and mixed vegetables. She'd made a Key Lime pie for dessert. She lit candles, opened a bottle of wine, and started a playlist she'd made just for the night. There was a cool breeze as the sun made its journey over the water. Riley looked around and decided everything was perfect. While she waited for Alex, she couldn't help but think she could get used to this. She didn't know how, but she fell deeper in love with Alex every day. The community had welcomed her, and she felt like a local now, not a tourist.

Alex made her way up the steps and looked around, taking it all in. "Look at all this! Riley, this place never looked so good."

"I'm glad you like it. I opened a bottle of wine, but you can have a beer instead if you want."

"No, I'll have wine with you."

Riley poured them both a glass and said, "Let's eat before it gets cold."

Alex came over and pulled Riley's chair out for her to sit. When she was seated, Alex placed a light kiss on her cheek. "Thanks for doing this," Alex said as she took her seat.

"I wanted to spend a beautiful evening with the woman I love. No need to thank me," Riley said serving them both.

While they were eating Alex said, "Sam called me this afternoon, and she and Rosie and Sasha will be here next week."

"That's wonderful," Riley said nervously.

"What's the matter, scared to meet the family? It's not like you haven't met them. I know it was on the computer but still you've chatted with them."

"I know," Riley said quietly.

"Babe," Alex said taking her hand across the table. "They are going to love you just as much as I do. Please don't worry."

"I just want them to like me. It's kind of a big deal, baby. When they've come to visit, you've never introduced them to a woman, much less one that's living with you."

"I get it, but I'm telling you Riley, they'll love you. When they see how happy we are, how can they not like you?"

"Okay. What all do we need to do to get ready for them? They're probably used to staying with you, so do I need to go somewhere else? Stay with Liz maybe?"

"Of course not! You're not going anywhere. This is our home now; you belong here. They always stay at the hotel you and Kara stayed at because there's a pool for Sasha."

But Riley was still focused on the earlier part of Alex's statement. "Our home?"

Alex smiled, squeezing her hand. "Yes, our home. This place never looked this good until you moved in. If you'll remember, it was a bit minimal, to say the least. You've made it a home, our home." Alex kissed the back of Riley's hand and looked into her eyes with love. "Now, could we not talk about my family anymore tonight? I'm on a date with the most beautiful woman in the world," Alex said smiling.

"There goes that charm of yours again. I thought we might dance a little and sit back and look at the stars," Riley said.

Alex stood, took her hand, and said, "May I have this dance?"

Riley stood and put her arms around Alex's neck. Alex pulled her close and kissed her softly on the neck. "Mm, this is so nice."

"You took me on so many dates when you were showing me the islands that I wanted to do something special for you. I know it's nothing like the places you took me, but I'm still learning my way around," Riley said.

"This is perfect. I love it up here. It's one of my favorite places along with our place at the park."

"Good. I'll make sure we do this more often."

"You know what I really love?" said Alex.

"What?"

"I love waking up with you curled next to me or on me, always touching me."

"It seems when you're near I have to be touching you."

Alex captured Riley's lips with her own, turning up the heat. "Those stars will still be there tomorrow, so I was wondering how this date ends?" Alex said breathlessly.

"Well, I thought I'd take you downstairs and show you how much I love you," Riley said.

"Hmm, that sounds like a perfect ending, but only if I get to show you the same."

"I'm sure that can be arranged," Riley said placing her hand on Alex's cheek. Alex leaned her head into her hand.

"I love you, Alex. So very much," Riley said kissing her softly. She grabbed Alex's hand and pulled her to the stairs, saying over her shoulder, "Come on, we can clean this up later."

8

Alex squeezed Riley's hand and said, "Breathe."

Her family's plane had arrived, and they were waiting for them to get through security.

"I'm just so nervous, Alex. I don't know what's wrong with me. Actually, I do. I want this to be the best visit ever for your sister and her family and I really hope they like me and think I'm good enough for you."

"You're rambling, darlin'. I'm the one that's not good enough for you, and they will tell you that as soon as they get to know you. Breathe."

Riley took a deep breath and held Alex's hand tight.

"Aunt Alex!" a little toddler screamed and ran toward Alex.

Alex swept Sasha into her arms and held her tight. "You've gotten so big! How did you do that? Stop growing! Do you hear me? Stop growing!" Alex said as Sasha giggled.

"Hi, I'm Samantha," Alex's sister said, extending her hand to Riley.

Riley took her hand and said, "It's so nice to meet you in person."

"Aunt Alex, she's yours. Do you know how hard it is flying with a three-year-old?" Alex's niece, Rosie, said lugging two overstuffed bags behind her. She walked up to Riley, dropped the bags, and hugged her. "Thank you so much for putting the sparkle back in my favorite aunt's eyes."

"I'm your favorite aunt because I'm your only aunt," Alex said pulling Rosie into a hug while holding Sasha.

"Hi, Sis," she said, handing Sasha to Rosie and hugging Samantha.

"Sasha, this is Riley," Rosie said introducing the lively little girl.

"Hi Wiley, Aunt Alex's gull-friend," she said, nodding her head up and down to her mom.

"That's right, Aunt Alex's girlfriend," Rosie emphasized. "She has a little trouble with her r's," she explained.

"Now that everyone has met, let's get your bags and get out of here," Alex said, tickling Sasha and putting her arm around Riley.

They picked up their luggage and headed for the ferry back to St. John. They made their way to the dock, and as they walked up to the ferry Alex grabbed Riley's hand, smiling, and winked at her. Riley was still nervous, but the touch of Alex's hand calmed her somewhat. She liked Alex's family, and they seemed to like her already.

"Mommy," Sasha said, pointing at the ferry. "Do we get to ride the big boat?"

"We sure do," said Rosie. They made their way to the top so that they all could get the beautiful views on the way to St. John.

Samantha stood near Riley. "Like Alex, you came here and liked what you saw, I guess."

Riley looked over at Alex holding Sasha and pointing

out things that made the little girl giggle. She answered Sam with a smile. "Yeah, you can say that. I do like what I see."

Sam said, "I can understand that. You must be something special because I've never, and I mean never, heard her talk about another woman since she's been here. And that's been sixteen years now, so I couldn't wait to meet you."

"That's what several people have told me, and I can't understand it to be honest because Alex is such a wonderful person. I'm feeling very lucky."

"Yeah, Alex is a good person, and she can have that effect on people."

"She's a charmer, that's what she is."

"Alex, charming? Are you kidding me?"

"She is!" Riley said, and they all laughed.

They made it to St. John and to their hotel. Alex and Riley left so her family could unpack, and they all decided to meet at Peaches later so they could see Liz. At the bar the patio was the best place to let Sasha run around, so they gathered there for food and drinks. Much laughter was shared, mostly at Alex's expense, as Samantha shared stories of their childhood.

Rosie pulled Riley aside and told her, "I've never seen my Aunt Alex this happy."

Riley said, "I've never been this happy either, so it goes both ways."

"I'm really glad you two found one another, and I hope it lasts. I'm not trying to be one of those people, but you're both happy, so figure it out," Rosie said matter-of-factly. "Sorry, was that too much?"

"No, it's just things happened so fast that we haven't talked much about what's to come. We're loving being together and getting to know one another better for now. But I don't want to talk about us, tell me about you."

"Well, we made this a girls' trip, so my husband, Seth, didn't get to come. Believe me he wanted to, but he'll wait and see Alex over the holidays. Maybe you can meet him then."

"What does your family usually do for the holidays?"

"Aunt Alex comes to visit before the holidays or after New Year's. That's a really busy time for her because people want to get away from the cold and come here. What does your family do?"

"My parents are retired and travel quite a bit, but they're always around for Thanksgiving and Christmas. My brothers and their families are also around unless they go to their in-laws. I have two nieces that I try to be a Super Aunt to, a lot like Alex. I don't see as much of them as I did because they are in college or working and have their own lives. I did call each of them and explain that I was staying here for the summer, and that got me lots of cool points with them," Riley explained. "I'm always expected to be the flexible one because it's just me. Sometimes that gets old."

Samantha overheard Riley and said, "I know what you mean. It's just me and Alex, and with her here, I'm the one they call."

"Don't say it like that, Sam," Alex joined the conversation. "It's not like I don't ever come home, and I do talk to them often."

"I know you do. Besides, they don't want to see me or Rosie anymore. They want to see that baby girl," Sam said laughing.

"I can see why," Riley said. Sasha was wearing down, so soon everyone said good night and Alex's family went back to their hotel.

The next few days were full of family fun time on the beach, shopping and swimming whenever Sasha wanted.

Some days Alex had to work. When that happened Sam and Rosie wanted Riley to come along on their adventures. By the end of their visit Riley felt like she was part of their family.

The night before they were to leave, Alex and Riley hosted dinner on the rooftop. Sasha wanted to see the twinkling stars so they hoped she could stay up long enough. She had so much fun watching the boats and the waves come to shore. Alex and Samantha went downstairs to get more food.

"Riley is really something, Alex," Sam said. "I hope you'll do everything you can to keep her around."

Alex laughed and said, "I hope to, but what do you mean exactly? Do you think I'm going to screw this up somehow?"

Sam said, "God, I hope not. Does she know about Texas?"

Alex looked down at her feet and shook her head.

"She deserves to know, don't you think?"

"Of course I do. I've been trying to tell her, but every time I think the time is right, something happens. I don't want to come home from work one day and jump right into it and say, 'Hey Riley there's something I need to tell you.'"

About that time Riley walked in and said, "What do you need to tell me?" She hoped this was it, Alex would finally tell her what was in her past.

Both Alex and Samantha's eyes went big. Sam rescued her sister by saying, "I was just talking to Alex about the holidays. That's what she was going to tell you."

Riley knew she had walked in on something. "O-kay? Let me take the food upstairs and you can continue your conversation. I didn't mean to interrupt."

"You didn't interrupt anything," Alex said placing a quick kiss on Riley's lips. But Riley could see that shadow in her eyes when anyone brought up the past. She grabbed the food and headed upstairs thinking she had given Alex enough time to tell her what was wrong. It was time they had a conversation, but she'd wait until her family went home.

When they were all back upstairs looking at the stars Alex tried to explain some of the constellations to Sasha. She pointed out the bear and the ram, and they took turns making the animal sounds. According to Sasha, they all had to do it, and the group started to get loud.

Rosie said, "Hey, everybody, we'd better quiet down a little. We don't want Aunt Alex to end up in jail again." As soon as the words left her mouth, Rosie knew she'd messed up. No one said a word. Riley looked at Alex with both eyebrows raised, asking the question silently.

Rosie tried to cover it up, but Alex said, "It's a good story. I'll tell you all about it someday."

"Right," Riley said. She knew there was something they were not telling her, but this wasn't the time, so she let it go.

They went back to the stars, but in the wake of Rosie's comment, the night had fizzled out. It wasn't long until they packed everything up to go back to the hotel. After they left Riley and Alex were in the kitchen cleaning up. There was obvious tension in the room. Riley went over and took Alex's face in her hands.

"Right there, I can see the shadow in your eyes. It's not always there, but it is now. It's time we have a conversation, don't you think?" she asked.

Alex closed her eyes and nodded her head.

"Not tonight, babe," Riley tempered her statement. "After your family leaves. I just want you to know that you can trust me with anything, Alex. I love you."

"I love you, too," Alex said quietly, with pain in her eyes.

Riley kissed Alex and took her hand and said, "Come on, we'd better get to bed."

When they got in bed, Riley took Alex in her arms until she was fast asleep, but Riley lay awake for some time wondering why Alex had waited so long to tell her whatever this was. It was obviously important and had something to do with why she was here in St. John. Riley couldn't understand why Alex didn't trust her. She couldn't get that out of her head because she knew she would trust Alex with anything at this point.

The next day Alex picked Samantha, Rosie, and Sasha up and brought them to the bar to say goodbye to Liz. They hugged Liz and said their goodbyes.

Riley said, "I'm going to stay here and let you have Alex to yourself for a bit. You've all been so nice to include me in everything, and I've loved it."

Rosie came over and gave Riley a hug. "You now know that I'm the big mouth of the family, but I'm so glad I got to know you and can't wait for you to come to Texas."

Sasha hugged Riley around the legs and said, "Wiley, come to my house and play. We have stars there, too, at night."

Riley picked her up and hugged her. "I'd love to come play at your house with you and see your stars, Sasha."

Samantha pulled Riley into her arms and whispered, "Give her a chance. I promise she's worth it."

Riley hugged her back and said, "I know she is."

"I hope to see you both sometime during the holidays, okay, Alex?" she said looking at both of them.

"Got it, Sis. We'd better get going," Alex replied. She kissed Riley and said, "I'll see you before I have to work tonight."

Riley nodded and smiled, working hard to keep it in place.

When they all left the bar, Riley took a seat. Liz came over to her and studied her for a moment.

"Would you like something to drink?" Liz asked.

Riley sighed and said, "I think I need a beer."

"Having to play family all week wear you out?"

"No, Liz, I fell in love with all of them."

"Then why do you look so worried?"

"You know why. Alex is keeping something from me, and I don't know why she doesn't trust me enough to tell me."

"She trusts you, Riley."

"Then what's going on? Anytime she talks about her past she gets a sadness in her eyes. It's been that way since the first night I met her. I know what kind of person she is, and I can't think of anything that could make me not love her. Surely, she knows that."

"Deep down she does know that but..."

"But what, Liz?"

The older woman shook her head. "It's Alex's story to tell. Trust in your love, and everything will be all right."

"Now you really have me worried." Riley shook her head and drank her beer.

* * *

Alex got back and ran upstairs to change before she went to work. Riley thought Alex had been crying.

"Are you all right, babe?" Riley asked, going to her.

"I always hate it when they have to leave."

Riley wrapped her in her arms and said, "I get it. They are absolutely wonderful."

Alex smiled and said, "I'll probably be late tonight, sorry."

"It's okay. I'll be right here waiting on you."

"Would you spend the day with me tomorrow? I'd like to go to the park, to our place."

"I'd love that."

"Okay," Alex said kissing Riley. "I'd much rather stay here, but I've really got to get down there."

"I know, baby. See you tonight," Riley said giving Alex a quick kiss.

Riley hoped Alex was finally going to talk to her tomorrow. If she didn't, Riley had decided that she would bring it up. This, whatever it was, had gone on long enough.

Alex did get home late that night, but Riley was there for her as always.

"Were you busy tonight?" Riley asked when Alex came in.

"Not too bad," said Alex, walking over to Riley and putting her arms around her waist. "I need something from you."

"Name it," Riley said.

"Tomorrow is for talking. Tonight I want to make love to you. I need to make love to you."

They held one another's eyes, and Riley answered with a slight nod. Alex kissed her passionately and led her to the bedroom without their lips parting. They both were out of their clothes by the time they made it to their bed. Alex laid Riley down gently, worshiping her with her eyes. She lay on top of Riley and lightly stroked her cheek, taking in every feature and burning into her memory so it would always be there. Even if her past tore them apart, she would always have tonight.

Riley broke the spell when she said softly, "I love you, Alex."

Alex slowly kissed and nibbled Riley's neck, ending at her ear, and whispered, "I love you, too, baby." This made Riley moan and want her more, but Alex took her time. She kissed her way down Riley's chest and took one nipple into her mouth, swirling her tongue around the tender bud, painstakingly slow. Riley's breath quickened, but Alex was in no hurry. She wanted to slowly and tenderly love this woman that had taken her heart. She finally reached the other breast as Riley ran her fingers through Alex's hair and writhed beneath her.

"Oh Alex, you're killing me," she panted.

Alex smiled but didn't increase her pace. She kissed and licked every inch of Riley's stomach, her lover's moans like music to her ears. When she finally made it between Riley's legs, she gently blew on her center and Riley's hips bucked. She was so close to being absolutely where Riley needed her, but she looked up and their eyes met. There was nothing but love in Riley's eyes for Alex. She lowered her head, and her tongue slowly moved through the wetness of Riley's folds. Riley continued to moan as Alex circled her bud. She took her tongue to Riley's opening and gently pushed in. Again Riley's hips bucked. Alex slowly ran her tongue from Riley's opening up around her bud torturing Riley with pleasure.

"I have to see your eyes," Alex said as she came back up Riley's body, kissing here and there. Her hand took up where her tongue left off. Riley closed her eyes, loving every moment.

"Look at me, Riley," whispered Alex. Riley opened her eyes and locked on Alex's. Alex's fingers entered her slowly, almost pushing Riley over the edge. Slowly, in and out, they found a rhythm as their love surrounded them. Their pulses raced, their breathing went faster and faster. When Alex put her thumb on Riley's bud, her legs stiffened, her fists were clenching the sheets, and then she threw her arms around Alex kissing her as she held on, riding the wave of her orgasm over and over. Riley didn't loosen her grip right away. She held Alex close, heart to heart, still panting in her ear.

When she was able to breathe more evenly, she eased her hold on Alex so she could look into her eyes. "That was…" Riley struggled for words.

Alex smiled. There were no words needed. She eased her head down on Riley's shoulder, and they lay like this wrapped up in one another's arms until they drifted off to sleep. Alex said a silent prayer for courage and one of understanding for Riley. They'd need them tomorrow. But tonight was as she hoped and would be burned in her memory no matter what happened.

9

It was a quiet drive to the park as Alex reached over and took Riley's hand. They looked at one another and smiled. Alex didn't think she had ever been this nervous or this filled with dread. This was either the end of life as she knew it, that's how much she loved Riley, or the beginning of a life filled with love, adventure, and laughter. Perhaps it was both. She so hoped for the latter. Liz had told them both on separate occasions to trust their love. Alex intended to do just that. Trust had been so hard for her even before coming to the islands, but she had to trust now. There was no other option. She couldn't continue to live without it.

As they pulled in and made the short hike to their spot, Alex laid a blanket on the ground. They both sat and she said, "Do you want to go for a swim?"

Riley just looked at her. A feeling of frustration was building inside, but she wasn't leaving this spot until Alex told her what she was hiding.

"You know, Alex, you, this, whatever we are, I think of as a whirlwind. We've had this whirlwind romance almost since I've set foot on this island," Riley said. "When I decided to stay we talked about trying to slow this down, but do we need to slow down? The love I feel for you in my heart, it's as if it's always been there, just waiting for us to find one another. And when we did, it didn't begin to blossom or bloom. It exploded into something big and all-encompassing immediately. And through this whirlwind, I thought you felt the same way because I've had no reason to be anything but open and honest with you. It's been easy to be who I am with you; I don't have to pretend I'm anything but me. The imperfect, 'not sure what she wants to do next,' person that is in love with you. So, no, I don't want to go swimming. I want you to trust me, trust us, trust this whirlwind enough to tell me what it is that makes you so sad."

Riley never took her eyes from Alex and waited.

Alex didn't look away. "I do feel the same way. I do trust you and feel I can be honest and open with you, but I haven't had that in my life for almost twenty years. I did something in the past that if you want to share a life with me will affect you, too. I wanted to tell you the day we came here for the first time, but that's when you told me that you were staying. As time went on I became more and more afraid because as much as I want to trust our love, I'm scared to death you'll leave me when I tell you." Tears sprang to Alex's eyes, and she took a deep breath. "I don't know where to start."

Riley rose to her knees and cradled Alex's head to her chest, trying to give her courage. "Start from the beginning," she said softly and sat back holding one of Alex's hands.

Hesitantly at first, Alex began. "When I graduated from college, I got a good job in a big firm in Dallas as a financial analyst. I was living the life. I worked a lot but also partied a lot. I made friends at work, and I had known a few people in town when I moved there. I dated and eventually had a relationship that lasted about a year. We never moved in together, though, and she broke up with me because I worked long hours. I knew it wasn't a forever thing, but still it stung." She held Riley's hand with both of hers now and paused to find courage to continue.

"True to the lesbian stereotype, I was on a softball team," she said. She tried to chuckle, but it came out more like a squeak. "The team was coed and made up of people from work and friends of friends. Some were straight, some were gay. After games we usually had some kind of party. After my girlfriend broke up with me, some of my friends on the team tried to set me up with their friends that would be at the parties."

With a faraway look in her eyes, she went on. "Sometimes everyone couldn't be at the games, so people would bring friends to sub. One girl that I didn't know very well brought her friend to sub one night when we were down several players. At the party after, this girl, Lindsey, and I flirted some. She came to the next game, and we all went to the house of one of my teammates after. There was a lot of drinking, and Lindsey and I ended up in one of the back bedrooms. We had sex, and I went home. This happened one other time, and then she didn't come around. I didn't think much about it because I was working long hours."

She took Riley's hand. "A week or two later she showed up at one of our games and told me that her parents didn't know she was gay but had found out she was hanging out with some of the gay players on the softball team and they were having a hard time with it. She said she wasn't going to be around for a while. I felt bad for her but didn't really think much about it because we really didn't know each other and people handle coming out to their parents all sorts of ways."

"A couple of days later I was at my apartment when a detective knocked on my door. He asked me if I knew Lindsey and if we'd had sex. I didn't lie because I knew that we hadn't done anything wrong. What I didn't know was that Lindsey was seventeen at the time. She looked like she was older and never said a thing. I incorrectly assumed that if she was out with us and drinking she had to be of age. Why would anyone bring her if she wasn't?" Alex looked at the sky and shook her head feeling so stupid, once again. Riley didn't say anything. She patiently waited.

"The next thing I knew he arrested me and took me to jail. I was so afraid and confused. I called a friend to bail me out. I had just enough time to go home, clean up, and make it to work. Needless to say, I couldn't believe how stupid I was and knew I needed a lawyer. Most of my friends rallied around me and wanted to help, but there wasn't anything they could do. Lindsey's dad just happened to be one of the big executives in the company where I worked. He was so upset about his daughter being gay that he wanted me sent to prison to teach her a lesson."

"You've got to be kidding me," Riley said.

"Not at all. I was twenty-eight years old and should've known better. My lawyer tried to get me the best deal he could with the DA. I was sentenced to ten years' probation and had to pay a fine. The worst part is that I have to register as a sex offender the rest of my life. I lost my job, and Lindsey's dad made sure I couldn't get another one in my field in Dallas. After paying my attorney, when I couldn't get anything else, I moved home because I was out of money. My parents didn't really know what to do. I was so ashamed and embarrassed and certainly didn't want the town to know, but the law took care of that."

"What do you mean?" asked Riley.

"Every so often they publish the names and addresses of the sex offenders in the town newspaper so everyone knows where they are. I found work, but it wasn't much. After about a year the city council decided to pass an ordinance that limited where sex offenders could go. Anywhere that children would be was off limits. Just about every community function and all the schools fell into this category. I couldn't even go to something as simple as the movies. I could go to church because they couldn't limit that." Alex paused so Riley could digest what she'd said.

"I tried not to draw attention to myself and I made a few new friends, but I was horrified they'd find out. Thank goodness they didn't read the newspaper. They would ask me to go to the movies or a town parade or things like that, and I always came up with an excuse. This went on for a year when Tina asked me to go to the Virgin Islands with her. She refused to let me become a hermit. I decided that a couple of weeks away might do me good, though it took almost all the money I had to go on the trip," Alex said, finding Riley's eyes. She couldn't read what was going on in that beautiful head of hers.

"When I got here I wandered into Peaches and immediately Liz came up to me and started a conversation. I cannot tell you how thankful I am for her. From that one conversation she took me in and gave me a purpose. I was able to transfer my probation and finish it. They don't have the ordinances here like they do in some towns and cities in the states. I do have to register once a year on my birthday, and law enforcement is understanding and discreet," Alex said wearily.

"Liz is the only one that knows besides the police, and I know she hasn't told anyone. I've never gotten close to anyone else because I'm so ashamed. That is, until you stepped into Peaches. I've wrestled with telling you because if you decide to stay, my sex offender status affects you, too. Someday it's going to come out, and I don't want you to go through the embarrassment my family did back in Texas. I just couldn't stand doing that to you," Alex said, her voice choking up as a tear spilled down her cheek.

"Are you sure no one else knows?" Riley said quietly.

"I know Liz wouldn't tell anyone."

"I believe you, Alex but, remember that man that yelled at us when we first came here?"

"Yes, I remember. I'm not sure but, I think someone must have found me on the sex offender website. It happened a couple of years ago. They wrote things on my car. Liz went to the police chief and everything died down."

So many emotions were running through Riley's mind and heart. She wanted to do nothing more than take Alex in her arms and comfort her, but there was still the fact that she took so long to tell her. Of course, Alex didn't want to hurt her, but that was going to happen in life. If something came up that Alex knew would hurt Riley, would she keep it from her the way she did this?

"I have a lot of questions, but first, I want to say that I know that was hard. Thank you for finally telling me," she said, then took a deep breath. "What I need from you right now, Alex, is to promise me that you will not keep something from me, even though you know it may hurt me. We can get through anything if we do it together as long as we both know everything."

"I promise." Alex then realized Riley said 'we', maybe they could get through this she thought.

They sat in silence for what seemed like forever to Alex. She held Riley's hand afraid to let go for fear she'd lose her.

Riley couldn't take the back and forth in her head any longer when Alex sat there so sad with tears in her eyes. She had a lot of questions, but one thing she knew in her heart was that she loved Alex. That was a good place to start.

"I've got to think, Alex."

Alex nodded. "I know you do," she said with a sad smile.

Riley reached over and smoothed her thumbs across Alex's cheeks, wiping her tears. She pulled her close and hoped she could feel the love surrounding them. They stayed that way a while, until Riley leaned back and tilted Alex's face up so she could look into her eyes.

"Would you take me back to your place?"

"Of course," she said standing up offering Riley her hand. They were walking back to the SUV, and Alex turned to Riley. She was afraid to ask but had to know.

"Are we okay, Riley?"

Riley looked at her. "We have a lot to talk about, but yes, we're going to be okay." She reached up, gave her a quick kiss, and they went to the SUV.

There were so many questions running through her mind. She knew recounting this was hard on Alex and that she needed a break. On the way back they decided to stop in the bar and check on things. As they walked in Liz looked from one to the other trying to read what happened.

"Is everything all right?" she asked.

Riley looked around the bar. It wasn't busy. "Do you think you could join us on the roof for a beer?" she asked.

"Sure. Let me grab a six pack—or do we need more?"

"We might need more. I have a lot of questions," Riley answered.

Liz grabbed the beer, noticing that Alex hadn't said anything, and hoped everything was all right. She didn't get a bad vibe, but she also knew this wasn't over. Liz had come to love Riley and would do anything to help them get through this.

They made their way up the stairs, and when everyone had a beer and had taken a seat, Riley said, "I'm very angry! I'd like to find this Lindsey and her father and beat the crap out of them! And I'm not really happy with you, Alex, for keeping this from me for so long." Riley looked from Alex to Liz. "And let me add that I would've thought you would have pushed her to tell me sooner."

Alex and Liz stayed silent, sensing that Riley wasn't finished.

After taking a few pulls on her beer, Riley said, "I've been teaching high school a long time, and the kids keep finding ways to look older. I've had several students, including my niece, that have easily acquired fake IDs and made it into clubs or other places they shouldn't be." She got up and started to pace. "What infuriates me is this girl probably had no idea how much trouble she could get other people in. Not just you but all the people that were there watching her drink, not having any idea she wasn't old enough."

"Yeah, but Riley, I should have been more careful and asked questions," Alex said. "I have to admit that I never even thought about her being so young. But, as the court and police continued to drive home, I was the adult. It still makes me sick to my stomach when I think about it. I was such a dumbass! I thought I was some hotshot financial wizard on her way up."

"That's because you were, Alex," said Liz.

Riley was trying to process everything Alex had told her

earlier and asked, "You finished your probation but you still have to register?"

"Yes, I have to register once a year on my birthday because I'm considered low risk. Some sex offenders," Alex cringed as she said the words, "have to register more often. The higher the risk, the more they report."

"But that didn't stop when you completed probation?"

"No, I have to do it the rest of my life. Imagine when I'm eighty and walking into police headquarters to register," Alex said, shaking her head.

"The rest of your life! That doesn't seem right. Shouldn't that stop after all these years?"

"No," Liz said sadly. "I was mad, too, when Alex finally told me. But I checked into the laws, and they are really fucked up. Someone like you shouldn't have to keep registering because you're not a danger. Others that are a danger should keep reporting, but by having people like you in the system, it dilutes it so much that they can't keep up with the bad ones. The laws need to be reformed, but it doesn't look like that will happen any time soon."

"That sucks. Alex, did you have any indication that maybe if all this hadn't happened you and this girl might have been together longer?"

"Not at all. We just hooked up, as terrible as it is to say."

"So, if she hadn't had this homophobic father, none of this would have happened?"

"Probably not, but I was still in the wrong."

Riley continued to pace, obviously mad. "I just can't believe it! He didn't want his daughter to be gay, so he had you locked up. I hope she's married to a woman and has two kids by now! I wonder if he'd have done the same thing if you'd been a man." Riley fumed. "And to ruin your career, too! Fuck!"

"I never saw her again. Some of my friends did, though, and said she felt horrible about it. She tried to get her dad to drop it, but after the initial charge was made it was out of his hands. He wouldn't stop anyway; that's why he put the word out so I couldn't get a job."

"I heard of something similar happening at my school," Riley said, trying to make sense of it all. "These kids dated and had sex when one had graduated and the other was still in high school. I never heard what happened to the boy, he was the older one, after they arrested him. I do know some of the teachers thought it was unfair because they were so close in age."

She got another beer and sat down.

Alex said, "I'm really sorry, Riley. You shouldn't have to deal with all this. That's what I was trying to explain to you earlier."

Riley stared at Alex. "So, it's all right for Liz to deal with this, but not me, the woman you're in love with?"

"I didn't mean it like that," Alex defended.

"Sure sounded like it. Makes me wonder if you'd have told me at all if your family hadn't let a few things slip."

Liz decided this would be a good time to leave. The couple obviously had more to discuss and didn't need her there. She could tell that Alex's past wasn't the problem. Riley was upset because she had waited so long to tell her. She hugged them both and left them on the roof.

Riley sat there with a sinking feeling in her stomach. She didn't like this at all. She knew that she loved Alex, but this idea that she didn't trust her enough to tell her this sooner was really eating at her. Is this what she had to look forward to? Would she always be pulling things out of Alex? All of a sudden, she was so tired and felt weighed down with all that had happened.

Alex didn't know what to say. She'd hurt Riley, and that was the last thing she ever wanted to do. Riley was so understanding about what happened, but she knew she was wrestling with how long it had taken Alex to be honest.

They sat in silence for a while; then Alex got up and sat down next to Riley on the couch and took her hand. She turned to face her and said, "I'm so sorry I hurt you. I know this is about how long I waited to tell you, not what actually happened."

Riley stared hard at Alex and finally squeezed her hand. "I know you didn't mean to hurt me. I need a little time to work through it, okay?"

"Of course." Alex hesitated, then asked, her voice shaking, "I'm not sure what that looks like. Do you need space?"

"Do you want me to stay with Liz?" Riley asked as her stomach fell even more.

"No! I just don't know if you need space or what. I'll do whatever you want, Riley."

Riley half smiled and released a breath she didn't realize she was holding. "What I want right now is for you to put your arm around me and hold me for a bit."

Alex didn't say a word. She took Riley in her arms. Riley laid her head on Alex's shoulder and wrapped her arm around Alex's middle. They stayed like this until the sun started to set; as the sky went from orange to red to gold to purple, they held on for dear life. So many thoughts and emotions ran through Riley's head, but finally she decided that she'd find a way through this with Alex. How that was going to happen she had no idea, and Alex would have to do her part. They were in this together, and it was time Alex understood that.

After a while Alex said softly, "I have dark days."

"What?"

"When my birthday gets near, I start to relive this all over again. All the shame and embarrassment come flooding back when I walk into the station to register." Alex took a deep breath. "You'd think after all these years it wouldn't be so hard, but it is."

Riley raised her head. She could see the starlight reflected in Alex's eyes along with tears. "I'm so sorry you have to go through that."

"That's how I found the cove at the park. I had registered, and it made me feel so bad I took a bike ride and ended up at the park. It was quiet that day, no one around, and I could hear the water. I saw the hint of a trail, and when I broke through the trees there was this little oasis. I sat there for a long time, and eventually I felt better and rode back to town. It's been a special place ever since; that's why I wanted to take you there. I feel at peace there." Alex took a breath. "That's what's so hard. It's a constant tug-of-war in my mind because the way I feel is all my own doing. If I hadn't been so stupid."

"You weren't stupid. Maybe naïve or not thinking, but it wasn't like you had sex with an underage girl on purpose."

"When I first met you and especially after that first night when I swear you grabbed my heart out of my chest. I was so happy, and then it hit me that I didn't deserve it."

"Why don't you deserve it? Alex, you made a mistake. You were punished and completed your probation. You deserve happiness as much as anyone."

Alex looked at Riley with such love. "But you don't deserve this," she whispered. "You deserve so much better."

Riley raised her eyebrows. "I don't deserve you? I don't deserve to be happy with you? I don't agree. It looks to me like we have both found our way to one another, and it's up to us to make our own happiness. Are you up for it?"

"I'd do anything to make you happy," Alex replied.

"We're a team, baby. We have to work together. No more of this who deserves what. No more secrets. And just because you think I'm not going to like something doesn't mean you keep it from me. Same goes for me. I took a leap and stayed here, and I wouldn't change a thing. It's hard not to be afraid, but I swear, Alex, if we trust each other, don't you think we can do this?"

"I do trust you! And I was afraid, but honestly, it's a relief that I finally told you. I know you're still mad at me, and I deserve..."

"Deserve?" Riley interrupted, raising one eyebrow.

Alex laughed. "Oops, don't give up on me, let me rephrase. You should be mad at me."

"That's better."

Alex looked thoughtful. "Thank you for talking about this. I keep it all inside, and I know that's not good."

"Then tell me about it. What was it like back home in Texas?"

Alex sighed. "It's like you walk around and know everybody is looking at you. They aren't, but that's how it feels. After the initial shock of moving home wore off, a childhood friend gave me a job. It felt good to be doing something, and my offender status wasn't always in the front of my mind. I made a few friends, and one of the guys had a daughter that played volleyball. He knew I used to play and asked me to help her."

Riley chuckled. "That doesn't surprise me at all that you played. I'm sure you were quite the jock."

Alex smiled. "I was hesitant to help at first, but he trusted me. I was able to show her a few things and went to all her games and sat with the family. This went on for a couple of years. I loved it, and that family became my friends."

"Did something happen?"

"Right after his daughter graduated, the city made the ordinance that restricted what I could do. I'm so glad she had graduated because I don't know how I would have explained that. I had gone to football and basketball games as well as school plays, and I couldn't do any of that anymore."

"That would be hard."

"It was, but I couldn't complain about it because, once again, it was my own fault. I was so tired of worrying about what people would think and not being able to do much but work. That's why I love working out so much. I could do that; I could sweat and not think about everything for a while. Then Tina was my lifesaver by insisting I go on this trip with her."

"What happened when you got here?"

"At first I spent a lot of time on the beach and went in to Peaches to drink. Liz could tell I needed help—she has a way about her. After I had been here for a week, I noticed one morning that I felt good. I was more relaxed. I wouldn't say happy, but I wasn't constantly sad either. That's when Liz offered me the job and I thought, why not? The restrictions weren't like they were back home, and the people here are so welcoming."

"I will agree that the people are welcoming—some more than others," Riley said, smiling before she planted a gentle kiss on Alex's lips.

"However, I thought life was good until this beautiful, redheaded, green-eyed goddess walked into Peaches and turned my world upside down."

"Goddess?" Riley said chuckling. "Just so you know, her

world was turned upside down, too. And babe, I understand that this is always going to be with you, but would you do me a favor?"

"Sure, name it."

"When you start to feel blue, come to me. I don't care what I'm doing or what's going on, come to me. We're doing this together now, and I'm here for you. I think what bothered me most was that I knew there was something you felt really bad about and you wouldn't let me help you."

"I realize that now. I thought, in my own way, that I was protecting you instead of letting you help me, but I don't want to do this alone anymore."

"You're not alone. But there's something you need to know, Kara called me right before your family got here to warn me"

"What do you mean warn you?"

Riley repeated her conversation with Kara and added, "I knew you would tell me, that's why I didn't press you and I didn't want to ruin your visit with your family."

Alex looked at Riley processing what she said, "You knew?"

"No baby, I didn't know what it was, but I knew there was something, I could tell."

"You could've done a background check then, but you didn't."

"Nope. There was no reason to. I trusted that you'd tell me, and you did."

"Do you think Kara and all your friends know?"

"I doubt it. When I told Kara I was going to wait, she agreed."

"But what happens when she finds out what it was?"

"It doesn't matter, Alex."

"It does Riley. These are your friends."

"Any friend of mine worth having will respect my decision to be with who I love."

Alex shook her head, "You hope they will, but…"

"Doesn't matter. I love you and with you is where I want to be."

Alex nodded and gave Riley a smile that didn't reach her eyes.

Riley took Alex in her arms and held her close. "Would you mind if we went to bed? I'm suddenly very tired. It's been quite a day."

Alex pulled back and said, "That would be fine with me. I think I'm emotionally and physically drained and couldn't talk about one more thing."

They walked hand in hand downstairs, went to bed, and fell asleep, legs and arms wrapped around each other.

10

The next few days they fell into a nice routine of work and play and felt closer than ever. Riley still had questions, and Alex answered the best she could. She wanted to understand the law and what was expected of Alex, but mostly she wanted to be supportive. Alex felt like a new person by being honest with Riley; knowing that Riley was by her side if this ever came out gave her great comfort and confidence.

Riley woke one morning with a brilliant idea, or at least she thought it was. She went looking for Liz knowing Alex had gone to St. Thomas to pick up supplies for the bar. She found Liz doing paperwork at one of the tables near the dance floor.

"Hi Liz, are you too busy for me to interrupt?" Riley said.

"Not at all. I welcome a reason to put this out of my mind for a bit."

"I want to do something special for Alex," Riley said taking a seat.

"Okay. What are you thinking?"

"Well, she told me that she dreads her birthday each

year because that's when she has to register. I've been trying to think of a way to make her birthday happy, and I think I've got it," Riley said.

"Tell me!"

"I want to throw her a surprise birthday party. Now. I know it's not close to her birthday, but we could celebrate it now and make it happy."

"That sounds fun!"

"I know she wouldn't go for a party if she knew, so that's where the surprise comes in. Would you help me?"

"Of course, I will. Where and when do you want to have it?"

"It would be easiest to have it here on the patio. That way we wouldn't have to close, and everyone from the bar could be here as well as friends."

"That would work. How about a week from today? Would that give you enough time to get it together?"

"I think so, if you help me with the invitations. Is this a good day of the week?"

"Yeah, Wednesdays aren't busy, and she usually goes to St. Thomas to pick up supplies, so she'll be gone during the day. That should give us time to decorate. I'll figure out some way to have her get back late enough that we can surprise her when she comes in," said Liz, liking the idea more and more.

"Oh, this is going to be fun!" Riley said.

"This is a really nice thing you're doing, Riley. I never knew that about her birthday. We usually celebrate, but now that I think about it, it's always been low key."

"How would you know if she didn't tell you? She's certainly not going to bring it up. I have been asking a lot of questions, and she's been good to answer. She's opened up a lot, and I'm so thankful she trusts me. That's too much to hold inside," explained Riley.

"I really hate this for her. You won't find a better person than Alex, but sometimes good people do bad things. That doesn't mean they're bad people, and this shouldn't follow her the rest of her life, but it will."

"It will, but she's not in it alone. She has us, and that makes a difference," said Riley.

Liz nodded and smiled. "Let's plan this party!"

* * *

A couple of days later Liz caught up with Riley on the beach. "Hey, would you like to go with me to the animal shelter? I'm volunteering for a few hours."

"I'd love to! I volunteered back in Florida. I didn't realize you had one here."

"We have a small one. You'd be surprised how many stray animals there are on the islands. The director is a friend, and there should be a couple of other people there to invite to Alex's party."

"Oh good. So far Alex doesn't have a clue. I have all the decorations hidden and ready to put up. I ordered food, too. That reminds me, I had a strange encounter while I was shopping for decorations."

"What happened?"

"I overheard a conversation between two women. They were talking about their kids and volleyball. Did Alex coach a team or something?"

"No, Beverly did. There was a beach volleyball league for middle and high school kids last spring and Alex helped her out a few times. Why?"

"I thought I heard one of them say Alex really helped

her daughter improve and the other said she wouldn't let Alex anywhere near her kid. When they both saw me, they stopped talking and walked away."

"Some people know about Alex. Most don't have a problem because they got to know her before they found out, but there are a few that do. I don't think Alex is aware of how many people do know."

"I didn't tell her about it because I wasn't sure they were talking about her but, I also knew it would make her feel bad."

"It doesn't happen often but, I hear things occasionally about her. People know not to say anything around me."

"When she first told me, her fear was that I would leave, but also it really bothers her that it affects me too. I was upset with her for not telling me sooner and made her promise not to keep things from me. But now I don't know what to do. If I tell her when something like that happens, she'll be upset, but then again, that means I'm keeping things from her."

"I see what you mean."

"There's obviously more to this than I thought."

"Are those second thoughts?"

"Not at all. My future is with Alex, I feel it in my bones."

"Why don't you talk to her? Tell her that you don't plan to share with her every time something is said because you know it will upset her and that's not good for either one of you."

"Ugh, I hate this. I'll talk to her."

Liz drove them to the shelter. As soon as she opened the car door Riley could hear a few random barks. Riley loved dogs and missed having one for the last year. She missed Benny, her Boston terrier that had died a year ago at age twelve. She had rescued him from the shelter, and he brought nothing but joy to her life.

They walked in the reception and office area and then through a door that led to the kennels. A woman that was around Riley's age, she guessed, was petting and playing with a tan-colored mutt that was loving every second of the attention. She looked up, and a big smile grew on her face when she saw Liz.

"Look who's here, Teddy! It's our favorite friend, Liz," she said, coming over to them.

"Hi Tessa, I'd like you to meet Riley James. Riley, this is Tessa, our shelter director."

Tessa stuck out her hand. "Nice to meet you, Riley. Liz has told me about you."

"Uh-oh," Riley said, shaking Tessa's hand. "I'm not sure if that's a good thing."

"It is. I've heard you're helping out around Peaches," Tessa replied.

"She's helping out all right. Just ask Alex!" Liz said with a laugh.

"Liz!" Riley said.

"What? There's nothing wrong with making people happy, and that's what you both are doing. I didn't say anything about *how* you put that silly smile on Alex's face," Liz said, still laughing.

Riley lowered her head.

"No big deal, Riley. I don't know anyone that loves to tease and flirt more than Liz," Tessa said pinning Liz with her eyes.

"Flirt. Why, Liz, whatever is Tessa talking about?" Riley asked, grateful the attention had been directed away from her.

Liz paused then said, "I'm not flirting. You simply take some of the things I say the wrong way."

"Why don't you go out with me and we'll find out?" Tessa said.

"You know why," Liz said softly and then added, "We're here to help. What do we need to do first?"

Tessa met Liz's eyes, seeming to decide to let it drop, whatever it was. Riley looked from one woman to the other, thinking she'd have plenty to ask Liz on the way back.

The shelter had room for around twenty dogs. There was a row of kennels that had wire mesh doors in the front and a doggie door at the back that allowed the dogs to go outside in a fairly large fenced area. Most of the dogs came inside when they heard Liz and Riley to see who the new voices belonged to. All of them wagged their tails, and some barked a greeting when Riley walked by. There were seven dogs and two cats currently residing at the shelter. Most of the dogs were medium to large mutts of various colors.

The three women pitched in to clean kennels and straighten up the storage area. Riley walked several of the dogs to give them more exercise than the fenced area allowed. Tessa joined her with another dog while Liz cleaned the room the cats were housed in.

"I'm glad I finally met you. Liz said you have really livened things up around Peaches," Tessa said as they walked the dogs.

"I don't know about that. Peaches seemed plenty lively the first time I walked in," Riley said, chuckling.

"It has a laid back vibe to me. That's what I like about it—that, and of course Liz."

"Did I hear you right earlier about Liz going out with you?" Riley asked. "Not that it's any of my business."

"That's all right," Tessa said. "And yes I've been trying to get Liz to go out with me, but she won't. She says it's because of the age difference, but maybe she doesn't like me that way."

"Really? I wouldn't think Liz would let something like that bother her."

"I've asked her a couple of different times, but she says she's too old for me. I'm not giving up, though."

"Too old? That's crazy. The more I get to know her, the more I wonder why she's alone."

"I know. She never goes out with anyone, and I've known her for quite a while."

"I've heard people say the same thing about Alex, but that sure has changed. Maybe it will for you and Liz, too," Riley said the matchmaking wheels turning in her head as they reached the shelter.

A woman was waiting when they went inside. "Hi Tessa," she said, "I see we have a new volunteer."

"Hi Karen, this is Riley. Riley, this is Karen," Tessa said, gesturing to each woman.

"Nice to meet you, Riley," Karen said, extending her hand.

Riley smiled. "Nice to meet you, Karen."

"You're new around here. Are you vacationing?"

"I am new, but I live here," Riley said, liking the sound of that.

"Welcome! I'd be happy to show you around," Karen answered.

"Thanks, that's nice of you, but I sort of have my own personal tour guide," said Riley, thinking of all the places Alex had taken her already.

"Oh, where are you living?"

"I live with Alex Adams," Riley responded.

"I heard Alex had a girlfriend," Karen said.

"That's right, Karen, so don't get any ideas," Liz said, walking up behind Riley.

"I was simply being friendly, Liz," said Karen.

"Yeah, I'm sure you were. The same way you'd like to be 'friendly' with all the lesbians on the Island," Liz said using air quotes.

"Come on, Liz, don't be like that."

"Be like what? You know it's true," said Liz.

"I can't help if I enjoy the company of a beautiful woman, and Riley, may I say, you are beautiful," replied Karen.

"Thank you?" Riley said not knowing what to think.

"If things don't work out with Alex, I'll be glad to show you around."

"See what I mean? Come on, Karen, you can help me with the cats," Liz said leading Karen inside the shelter.

"That was weird," Riley said to Tessa.

"Yeah, Karen is a little different, but she volunteers here all the time and I need the help," said Tessa. "She's really harmless. I think she's just a little lonely. Come on, we have two more dogs to walk."

When they got back and put the last two dogs in their kennel, they found Liz and Karen talking to someone new.

"Hey Tess, this is Sherry. She wanted to look at the dogs we have up for adoption. Sherry, this is Tessa, the shelter director."

"Hi Sherry, I'd be glad to show you the sweethearts we have here," Tessa said leading Sherry through the door to the kennels.

"I'll help," Karen said following them.

"Hopefully someone is about to have a new home," Liz said.

"That would be awesome! But hey, what's this about

Tessa asking you out and you not going?" Riley said.

"That would be none of your concern," Liz said looking away.

"Oh, no, you don't. You're the one that told Alex she needed to take a chance on me. So, what's stopping you from doing the same thing, Liz?"

"It's not that simple, Riley. Tess and I have known one another a long time. We have a great friendship, and I don't want to ruin that. Besides I'm too old for her."

"What do you mean, too old? That's crazy! You're not too old to have a good time, share a meal, share some laughter," Riley said.

"I don't mean it that way, Riley. I mean I'm too old for Tess. She's younger than you, for god's sake."

"So?"

"So, first I can't imagine why she would want to go out with me," Liz said, holding up her hand to keep Riley from speaking. "And what if we do and things progress? I don't want Tess having to take care of an old woman someday. If we leave things as they are, then we get to continue our friendship and that is important to me."

Riley nodded, understanding Liz's reasoning. "I get what you're saying, Liz. But you could be selling Tessa short. Maybe that's what she'd want to do. We don't know how long we have together with anyone."

"I realize that, Riley, but if I ever held her back from anything, which my age could do someday, it would break my heart," Liz said.

Riley knew she needed to drop this for now. "Let me just say this, and I'll let it go for now. I've taken a pretty big chance here, and it is giving me more joy than I've ever known. If for some reason this doesn't work with Alex, I won't regret it because my heart has never been this full."

Tessa walked into the room with Sherry and Karen, looking from Liz to Riley. She said quietly, "Is everything all right?"

Liz smiled and said, "Sure, Tess, everything is fine. Did you find a dog, Sherry?"

"I think maybe I have. I'm filling out an application and bringing it back tomorrow," said Sherry.

"That's great!" Riley exclaimed. While Tessa got Sherry the necessary paperwork Riley said, "Hey, we're having a surprise birthday party for Alex on Wednesday, and I was hoping you all could come."

Tessa looked up and said, "Isn't Alex's birthday in November?"

"It is," Liz said, "but you know how Alex feels about parties and being the center of attention, so Riley is throwing a surprise party for her birthday early!"

"How fun!" Karen said. "I'll be there. Do we need to bring anything?"

"No, just yourself. Meet on the patio at Peaches around five. Come through the beach entrance. And don't tell!" Riley explained.

Sherry left to complete her paperwork, and Karen left shortly after. Liz and Riley helped Tessa feed the dogs and finished their chores while she closed everything.

"Thanks for helping out today, Riley," Tessa said as she walked them to the car.

"I loved it! I'll be back. Call me anytime you need help," Riley said, getting into Liz's Jeep.

Tessa walked around the Jeep with Liz and opened her door. "Thanks again for the help and for being someone I can count on, Liz." Liz got in, and Tessa closed the door putting her hands on the windowsill. "I'll see you later for that drink you owe me. I'm collecting tonight." She patted Liz on the arm, winked, and stepped back.

"Sounds good, I'll see you then." Liz started the Jeep and began to drive off. After only a moment she turned to Riley and said, "Not a word."

Riley could see Liz meant business. She'd be quiet for now, but if she could do anything to help Liz find the happiness she and Alex had, then she was going to do it.

* * *

Everything was set for the party. Alex was on the supply run, Riley had picked up the food, and she and Liz were almost finished with the decorations. She hoped Alex would like it; she so wanted her to have a birthday without the dread or sadness that her past would bring.

"Alex just called and said she would be a little late. There was something wrong with the order. Imagine that," Riley said chuckling.

Liz laughed and said, "I had them delay things just a bit so we could have plenty of time to get ready. They loved the idea of surprising Alex."

"Nice touch," Riley said, looking around the patio. "Everything looks great, and we're ready with time to spare. People should be here soon, and we can get this party started!"

"It does look nice out here. Alex is going to be so surprised," said Liz.

"I sure hope this doesn't backfire. I want her to have a happy birthday without the other drama for once, but she may not like surprises."

"She'll like this one, especially given why you did it," Liz assured Riley.

"This place looks awesome!" Tessa said, walking onto the patio.

"Hi Tessa, thanks, we're ready. All we need are people and Alex," Riley said.

"Hi Tess, how are things at the shelter?" Liz asked.

"Everyone is fine. They'll be happy to see you both tomorrow."

"I wanted to ask you, Tess, is that invitation to dinner still open?" said Liz.

"It certainly is," Tessa said with a hopeful look in her eye. Riley looked on, unable to hide her surprise.

"I would like to accept then," Liz said.

"I'm so glad! Not that it matters, but has something changed your mind?" Tess said.

"Well, you have worn me down. You just wouldn't stop asking me out. Besides, someone may have made me look at things in a different way," Liz said glancing at Riley.

Riley's eyebrows rose. "Who, me?"

"You may have said a few things, I'll leave it at that," Liz said.

"Thanks, Riley! I've been trying to get Liz to have dinner with me for months," Tessa said. Then she turned to Liz and said, "How about tomorrow? Too soon?"

Liz laughed. "No, that's fine. We can make plans later. We have a party to throw first."

Guests had begun to arrive, and it wouldn't be long until Alex got back. Riley was beginning to get nervous, but she also couldn't wait to see Alex. Her phone pinged in her pocket.

Alex: I'm at the dock. Be home when I get things put away.
Riley: Meet me on the patio. I missed you!
Alex: Missed you too, baby. See you soon.

"Okay, everyone! Alex just texted and said she's at the

dock, so she'll be here soon. Get ready," Riley told the group. She felt like her heart was going to beat out of her chest.

* * *

Alex walked in the bar and saw Max walking toward her. "Hey Alex, you made it back."

"Finally! I've never had to wait that long."

"I'll unload. Riley needs you on the patio."

"Oh, okay. Thanks, Max." Alex walked over to the patio door and nodded at a couple of people at one of the tables inside. When she walked outside all she heard was "SURPRISE!" She looked around and saw a banner that said, "Happy Birthday, Alex" and that the patio was full of her friends. Then she saw Riley walking to her with a big smile.

Riley saw the confusion on Alex's face. She took Alex's face in her hands and said, "Happy Birthday, Alex."

Alex kept smiling as she said, "But it's not my birthday, Riley."

"It is your birthday. Your special day to celebrate you and nothing else," Riley said, staring into Alex's eyes and hoping she understood.

Alex heard what Riley said and knew there was more to it, and then it hit her. Riley was having a birthday party for her on a day that she didn't have to register with the local law enforcement. There would be no sadness, none of her past creeping in to spoil it, just happiness. Alex looked at Riley with understanding and nothing but love in her eyes. She pulled her close and kissed her with all the love she was feeling. She wanted to keep kissing her and never stop, but then her friends' applause, laughter, and whoops brought her back to reality.

"Here, you get to wear the special birthday tiara," Liz

said, coming over and placing it on her head. Alex looked around and saw that everyone was wearing a party hat.

"Thanks, everyone! I'm definitely surprised!" Then her friends came up and gave her a hug or patted her on the back, but she never let Riley get far away. After everyone had something to drink and the music started, Alex pulled Riley aside.

"This whole party is so sweet and unexpected. Thank you."

Riley looked into her eyes and realized she'd never be able to leave this person that had her heart. They were going to have to find a way to be together, Riley was as sure of that as the beautiful sunset that was beginning over their shoulders.

Riley beamed. "I love you, Alex."

"Oh Riley, I love you, too," Alex said.

"Come on, it's time to cut the cake," Liz called to Alex. Alex knew she'd enjoy the party, but she couldn't wait to get Riley upstairs and thank her properly for this special day. She never dreamed her life could be this happy and she knew it was because Riley lived in it.

11

Riley had been struggling with a decision. After their talk about being a team and not keeping things from one another, she knew she needed to sit down with Alex and tell her what she was thinking.

One morning after they'd been on a run Riley said, "Babe, I need you to sit down with me and have a talk."

"Uh-oh, is something wrong?"

"Nothing is wrong. I need to run something by you and get your thoughts on it."

"Okay, I'm all ears."

"Even though I'm retired and don't have to go back to Florida, I do still have a house there. I was thinking that I should rent it or maybe even sell it."

"Makes sense. I realize this has been a whirlwind, as you like to say, but my life is full now that you're in it. I'm living this love you've given me. But…"

Riley's stomach fluttered, "But?"

"But I don't expect you to give up your life in Florida."

"What do you mean? I'm retired. It makes sense for me to relocate here, you own a business."

"I know that, but you have family and friends in Florida."

"I'm not understanding."

"What I'm trying to say is that if you want to go to Florida or move somewhere else, I'll go with you. Just because I have a business doesn't mean I can't leave. I love you Riley, I want to be where you are."

Riley thought her heart would burst in her chest; it was so full of love for Alex. "You'd do that for me, for us?"

"I sure would. I love our life."

"I do too. That means so much, but let's stay here."

"If that's what you want."

Riley smiled and kissed Alex tenderly, "I do, and I want to sell my house. I'll call Kara and see if she knows a realtor, she has connections everywhere."

"That doesn't surprise me," Alex said chuckling. "I'm going to shower."

Riley grabbed her phone and called Kara.

"If it isn't my BFF in paradise," Kara said answering.

"Hey, how are you?"

"Probably not as good as you but, making it."

Riley chuckled, "Maybe you need to think about joining me here in paradise."

"Is it still paradise, are you still love birds?"

"I can't imagine life without her. What did I do before we walked into Peaches?"

"You'd think the newness would wear off, but my god, you're getting sappier the longer you stay there."

Riley laughed.

"So, I'm guessing Alex came clean on whatever was in her past?"

"She did." Riley recounted Alex's story and explained why she took so long to share it.

"Wow, what a deal. Are you sure you want to take this on? It changes your life too, Riley."

"I know. I've thought it through and even experienced some of it."

"What do you mean?"

Riley explained the looks she sometimes noticed and the women at the store.

"Damn, no wonder Alex didn't want you to know. But Riley—"

Riley stopped Kara, "No buts Kara, I'm doing this. I love Alex and this is part of it."

"But a sex offender! Just the stigma alone from the label."

"Look, I've made up my mind, I'm staying and that's actually why I called you in the first place. I want to sell my house."

"Sell your house!"

"Yep, I'm making a life here with Alex so I don't need a house in Florida."

"But what if things don't work out. You'll need a place to stay."

"Everything is going to work out, Kara. I don't need the house. And by the way, Alex did offer to move to Florida with me."

"Well, that's something! You're really doing this, aren't you?"

"We're really doing this."

Kara was quiet a moment then said, "I'm trying to think of all the things I'm supposed to say to talk you out of this, but I've got nothing."

They both laughed then Kara said, "What about Sara, she knows and what about your family. Are you going to tell them?"

"I'll talk to Sara. I'm sure she told Julie."

"She probably did tell Julie but, I'm not so sure she said anything to anyone else. I saw Kim last week and she asked how you were doing. She didn't mention anything about Alex's past. What if your other friends aren't as open minded as I am?"

"What do you mean?"

"They might not want to be around Alex and what about your brothers? You know good and well that they are not going to be as understanding."

"My friends have already been around Alex even if it wasn't very long and seemed to like her. And it doesn't matter! It doesn't make her a different person than you knew before."

"Listen to yourself. You're already defensive and haven't talked to anyone yet."

Riley sighed, "I am defensive because Alex is a good person and wasn't treated fairly."

"*You* think she wasn't treated fairly that doesn't mean everyone else won't think it was fair."

"I love her, Kara," Riley said quietly. "All of her past, present, and future."

"Okay, I have a realtor friend. I'll get her on it." With that Kara caught Riley up on their other friends and promised to visit soon.

* * *

Riley was sitting in a lounger on the beach, looking out at the water when Alex walked up and kissed her cheek. The kiss was welcome but it startled her.

"Wow. Why so jumpy, babe?" Alex said sitting at her feet.

"I just got off the phone with Kara. She found a buyer for the house."

"Really! I thought you were listing it?"

"I was. She was at a party, imagine that," Riley said chuckling. "Anyway, she was talking to a friend that had a friend looking for a house in that area. She showed them the house, and they loved it. They want to buy it."

"That's great! It's almost like it was meant to be," said Alex. "But why do you not look happy?"

"Well, I have to go back. I need to pack up my things and do something with all my stuff. I'm a little overwhelmed."

"I can see why. I didn't think about all your stuff. This is happening so fast."

"I know. Kara is going to see if the buyers want any of my furniture. If they do, I'll still have to pack up my clothes and other things."

"When would you leave?" Alex said, not liking the idea of Riley leaving but knowing she had to.

"Soon. It'll take two to three weeks to do the closing on the house, but it'll take me some time to pack everything up and decide to store it, sell it, or bring some here with me."

"What can I do to help?" Alex asked.

"You know, you could come with me."

Alex thought about it and nodded. "Let me talk to Liz."

Riley sat up excited. "Really?"

Alex smiled. "Yes, really. I do own the bar if you'll remember."

Riley scooted down and hugged Alex tight. "That would make it so much better if you came with me."

"Okay. Figure out when we need to leave and I'll talk to Liz," Alex said kissing Riley.

"I love you, Alex."

Alex laughed. "I love you, too, Riley."

Riley went to work making all the arrangements. They left a week later; the plan was for Riley to stay two weeks and get the house and her things settled. Alex would be staying the first week with her and help her pack up before going back to St. John.

Kara picked them up at the airport and took them to Riley's old house. Alex was nervous. Meeting Riley's family for the first time face to face; she wanted them to like her. But with her past always looming in the background it made times like these even more anxious.

"So, when is the big family meet?" Kara asked.

"I'm sure somebody will show up tonight, but we're supposed to see Mom and Dad for lunch tomorrow. They're leaving for their next trip the day after."

"Are you nervous, Alex?" Kara asked, teasing.

"You could say that."

"Oh baby, it'll be fine," Riley said. "My folks know what the deal is and they're happy for me even though so much has changed in such a short time."

"You can say that again," added Kara. "But, she's right, Alex. Her folks are good people, and they're going to love you."

"Why do you say that?"

"Because Riley loves you. She's their baby girl, and what she wants, she gets."

"Oh really? I don't remember you saying anything like that, baby," said Alex.

"Because that's not necessarily true. They're glad I found someone; now they won't worry about their poor little daughter being alone while they travel the world," Riley said, chuckling.

"Hmm, I'm not sure how to take that."

"What she means is that her parents trust her judgment.

Believe me, they know Riley is careful about who her friends are and who she lets in her bed," Kara said matter-of-factly then laughed at the look on Riley's face.

Before either one could say anything Kara pulled up into Riley's driveway and said, "Okay, you two, I'll leave you to it. Let me know when you want me here to help you pack up."

"I will. Thanks for picking us up, Kara."

"Any time. Welcome to Florida, Alex."

"Thanks."

Riley had a beautiful house. It was a two-bedroom bungalow with a nice yard and just right for her. That is, until she went to the Virgin Islands for a wedding. As she looked around she knew there were things she would miss, but she felt a freedom in selling it and most of her things to continue this adventure with Alex.

"This is a great house. It fits you. Are you sorry you have to sell it?"

"Not at all. It's just a house. You are my love, and our place back home is perfect for us. I know that sounds sappy, but I seem to have turned into a sappy, romantic woman in love."

"There's no shame in that. I love your romantic side. It's brought out the romantic in me."

Riley kissed her. "We'll be sappy together and ignore our friends making fun of us. They're just jealous anyway."

Alex kissed her back. "There's nothing I'd rather do than kiss you the rest of the day, but we have lots to do in a short time. Put me to work."

Riley did just that, starting in the guest room and going through closets to donate clothing she didn't plan to take with her. She talked to her mom, who told her that she had told the rest of the family to leave them alone this first night. They got quite a bit done with piles for donating, a pile for her sisters-in-law to go through, and a few things Riley was taking with her.

"You have some great artwork that would look really nice in our place," Alex said, looking around the living room.

"I hadn't really thought about taking any of it, but you think it would?"

"I do. Besides, you need some of this so it'll feel like your home too. I know you've changed some things there, but I really like these," Alex said pointing to a couple of prints Riley had hung over the couch.

"Okay. Why don't you go through and pick some things that you like or think would work back home and we'll decide together?"

They continued to work on making groups of items to stay, donate, or take. Riley ordered takeout, and they took a break to eat. By late that evening they'd had enough for one day and sat on the patio drinking beer and relaxing before going to bed.

When they went into the bedroom, Riley threw Alex down on the bed and straddled her. "There's something I've wanted to do ever since you told me you'd come with me."

Alex looked at her with both eyebrows raised. "Oh, there is?"

"Yes, I want to make love to you in my bed." Riley leaned down and kissed Alex hard. When she raised up, she took her shirt off and threw it across the room. She unclasped her bra, tossing it aside, too. "Sit up, you have on too many clothes," she said, taking Alex's shirt off and unclasping her bra.

"And if this bed could talk, would it tell me stories?" Alex said teasing.

"Don't mess with the mood, babe."

"I wouldn't dare," Alex said taking Riley's face in her hands and kissing her. Before Riley knew what had happened Alex had flipped them and was on top of her, taking her pants and panties off in one motion.

"Wow, what's happening," Riley said, giggling.

"Let me show you what's happening," Alex said, crushing Riley's lips with her own.

Later Riley lay flat on the bed trying to regain her breath. "I assure you this bed has never seen anything like that."

Alex chuckled. "That's good to know."

"That didn't turn out anything like I imagined," said Riley, her breath finally returning.

"And how did you imagine it?" Alex said.

"Let me show you," Riley said, crawling on top of Alex.

* * *

On the way to lunch the next day Alex said, "We may have to find a way to take that bed back with us."

"You like that bed, do you?"

"I like what happens in that bed," Alex said, wiggling her eyebrows at Riley. "Watch the road."

Riley laughed and reached for Alex's hand, thinking she was the luckiest woman in the world.

Lunch with Riley's parents went great. They were so nice to Alex and seemed to be reassured by how quickly their daughter had upended her life after meeting and talking with her. They promised to include the Virgin Islands in their travels and come visit soon.

Alex met the rest of the family at Riley's parents' that night for dinner. She was nervous when they walked in but was quickly put at ease by meeting Riley's nieces, Rachel and Amy, who just finished their second summer semester at college. They both wanted to know everything about the island and how Alex and Riley met.

"So, I know Aunt Riley walked into your bar and that's how you met, but what happened next?" Rachel asked.

Riley looked at Alex and said to Rachel, "Let's just say that we hit it off immediately."

"Well that's obvious, but I know there's more to it," Amy said looking at them both.

"We had a really good time that first night, and they came back the next day and I managed to get an invite to Kim and Kerry's wedding. After that…" Alex said but was interrupted by Rachel.

"After that you couldn't keep your hands off one another, and here you are!" Rachel exclaimed holding her hands up and arms out in a "what else" gesture.

Riley looked at Alex, then at Rachel and Amy, and said, "Well, that pretty much sums it up."

"Wait, you're not going to tell them about the ferry?" said Alex.

"What about the ferry?" asked Rachel. "Come on, Aunt Riley, what happened?"

Riley looked at Alex, narrowing her eyes, and whispered, "Are you trying to make me look bad in front of my nieces?"

Alex shook her head and whispered back, "That's not possible, you never look bad."

"I don't think your charm is going to get you out of this one," Riley said and turned to her nieces. "Well, I didn't know that the ferry doesn't run at night. And I got separated from the rest of the group and they took the ferry without me. When I went back to Alex's bar to find them, they were gone and I missed the ferry."

Alex jumped in and said, "That's when I got to rescue her, or she probably wouldn't have come back the next day."

"You knew I was coming back the next day," Riley said, smiling.

"So what happened?" said Rachel.

"How did you rescue her?" said Amy.

Riley looked at Alex with both eyebrows raised. Alex said, "I helped her find a place to stay. So, she had to come back the next day to thank me. And that's what happened."

Rachel and Amy looked at one another, sensing there was more to it. Rachel said, "You know, it would be the perfect story if the place Alex found you just happened to be hers."

Riley and Alex looked at one another and didn't say a word.

Amy laughed and said, "I knew it! Aunt Riley, you're still a little hottie!"

"Yeah, you are!" Rachel chimed in.

"I'd have to agree with you both," Alex added.

Riley's cheeks were beginning to turn red when her sister-in-law Jodie came in and said, "Ease up on your hot aunt. You're embarrassing her."

"We're not embarrassing her. I'm going to get the full story out of you someday, Aunt Riley, just sayin'," Rachel said, giving her aunt a big hug.

"Me too," said Amy. "You're our hero! Who goes off for a vacation, finds a girlfriend, and moves there?"

"Don't get any ideas, you two," Riley said, turning to Jodie and Jenn, her other sister-in-law. "Have I lost all my credibility with them now? Am I a bad role model?"

They all laughed. "Of course you're not," Jenn said, patting Riley on the back.

Riley's brothers Kevin and Keith walked in. Kevin said, "What's so funny? Are they picking on you, little sister?"

Before Riley could answer Keith said, "You have to admit this is all moving a little fast." Alex noticed how Keith looked at her, giving her an uneasy feeling.

"It is fast, Alex and I will be the first to admit it, but you all know I was looking for a change this summer," Riley said to the group.

"A change? This seems to be a lot more than a change," Keith replied.

"Oh, ease up, Dad," said Rachel. "This is one of the coolest things that has ever happened to this family."

"It sure is! This is the best story!" Amy added.

Alex had been quiet through this. She didn't like the vibe she was getting from Keith and decided to speak up, "If we were twenty-five years younger, I'd agree that this is too fast, but Riley and I aren't kids. Why would we waste time now that we've found one another?"

Riley looked at Alex and beamed.

Alex continued, "I understand that you don't know me, but all I want is for Riley to be happy, which I know is the same thing that all of you want."

"You're right, that is all we want, and it's obvious you do make her happy, Alex," Jodie said.

"And I'm glad we got to meet you before Riley moved," Kevin added.

"I am, too, but, you will all come visit, won't you?" Alex asked.

"Well, maybe not all at once," Riley said putting her arm around Alex's waist.

They all laughed.

"We're going first!" Amy and Rachel said together.

The rest of the night went well as the group welcomed

Alex. They all had stories to tell about Riley that were funny and sweet. By the end of the night Alex felt like one of the family, but she still had an uneasiness about Keith. He was nice to her, but sometimes she would catch him looking at her as if he wanted to say something. She decided she must be imagining it because Riley didn't seem to notice.

12

Before Alex had to leave, Kara decided to throw a going-away party for Riley. She invited her family, a few friends, including most of the ones who had been at the wedding that brought them to the Virgin Islands at the beginning of the summer. It was a welcome relief from all the packing and sorting at Riley's house.

Alex looked around the room and saw that she knew just about everyone. She liked getting to know Riley's family and friends. They would always be part of their lives, and thank goodness they liked her.

Riley's nieces made her think of Rosie, and she liked being around them and listening to their stories. She watched Riley from across the room. She was having a good time, but occasionally she would look up to find Alex and meet her eyes with a smile. Alex needed another beer, and Kara had a generous supply on the patio out back.

"Can I get you one?" Keith asked digging around in the ice chest.

"Sure, what you're having is fine," Alex replied.

Keith opened a beer and handed it to her.

"Thanks." She paused for a moment. "Look, Keith, I understand and appreciate that you're looking out for your sister, but I wanted to assure you that all I want for Riley is happiness."

"I want the same. But you have to admit, this has all happened so fast."

"I know it has, but I think the reason for that, if you don't believe in love at first sight, is because we know what we want from this relationship and aren't afraid to go for it. We have a lot of living to do, and we want to do it together."

"Love at first sight," Keith mumbled. "You are perfect for one another. You're both romantics."

Alex laughed. "Don't knock it till you try it."

Riley walked up, putting her arm through Alex's, and said, "What's funny?"

Alex said, "Your brother here doesn't seem to be much of a romantic."

"You've got that right."

"Well, maybe he should try it. I highly recommend it," Riley said.

Keith moaned. "See? You're perfect for one another, both romantics." He walked off shaking his head.

Riley stood in front of Alex, looking into her eyes. "Everything all right?"

"Everything is fine, except there is one thing I could use from you."

"And what is that?" Riley said, putting her arms around Alex's neck.

"This." Alex leaned in and kissed her. Before Riley could deepen the kiss Kara walked onto the patio.

"Oh, come on, lovebirds, can't you keep your hands off one another for a minute?"

Riley beamed as she pulled away. "It is hard sometimes."

"Can I get you a beer?" Alex asked Kara.

"Yes, you can and one for Kim, too."

"Coming right up. I'll take this to Kim for you," Alex said, opening a beer for Kara.

"Thanks, I need to speak to your woman anyway."

"My woman? Okay, I'm going to leave now," Alex said giving Riley a look.

Alex saw Kim going into the kitchen and followed with her beer. "Kara said you were ready for another," Alex said, handing Kim a beer.

"Thanks."

"So how is married life?"

"I've got to tell you it's amazing. Maybe you and Riley should check it out."

Alex nodded and smiled.

Kim said, "There's something about making promises in front of your family and friends that solidifies it. We had made promises to one another long ago, but this feels more lasting, like nothing will come between us. It's the best!"

"That sounds wonderful," said Alex.

"I'm telling you it is. It makes me even more grateful for the people that stood up and fought for the right to marry. And for those brave women, like Edie Windsor and Thea Spyer, that were trailblazers and made sure that we have rights like anyone else. I'm so thankful for those people."

"I know, Riley and I have talked about the strength and courage those women had. Maybe that's what I need, a little of their courage to take the next step."

"What's stopping you?" Kim asked.

"Actually I have thought about it. Riley has made so many big decisions the last couple of months, and I didn't think the timing was right. But after she gets back and settles in, I'm planning to ask her to marry me."

"Ah!" Kim's eyes shone as she squeezed Alex's arm. "I think that's great!"

"Shh," Alex said, looking around. "Riley doesn't know."

"Don't worry, I won't tell anyone, but I'd better get an invitation."

"Oh you will. By the way, I wanted to thank you for choosing the Virgin Islands for your wedding and bringing Riley into my life."

"You are very welcome. I may have gotten her to that bar, but the rest was the two of you making the magic happen."

They both laughed.

Kim said, "Can I ask you a question, Alex?"

"Sure."

"You were talking about all the decisions and changes Riley made, and I was wondering-- if Riley wanted to come back here, would you come with her?"

Alex smiled. "In a heartbeat. I'd follow her anywhere, but she happens to love St. John."

Kim smiled, nodding her head. "That's good to know."

* * *

The next morning Alex packed her things. She had helped Riley a lot even though she had plenty left to do the following week. Alex couldn't help being a little sad leaving Riley in Florida. It was crazy to think about, but in two and a half months they hadn't been apart for even a night. That thought made Alex smile, but it also made her miss Riley and she hadn't even left yet.

Alex had been thinking about asking Riley to marry her for a while now and talking to Kim the night before and saying it out loud made it feel real. She couldn't believe that the thought didn't scare her. The life she led before Riley

James was one of fear and hiding, but that was gone. Riley would never know how much confidence and comfort she had given Alex. Listening to Kim last night made her want those things forever. She never thought she would find someone that would understand and want to have those things with her. Now she had a new life in her reach, and it was like a dream. That's how she thought of it: she was living a dream.

"I'm not looking forward to this next week," Riley said, walking into the bedroom.

"It shouldn't be too bad. We got a lot done, and Kara said she'd help you with what's left," Alex said zipping up her bag and setting it on the floor.

"I don't mean that. I'm not looking forward to being without you," Riley said.

Alex looked up and smiled. "Aw, you're downright adorable when you pout." She walked over and took Riley's face in her hands. "I don't like it either, baby. I can't tell you how much I'm going to miss you." She placed a soft kiss on Riley's lips.

"Is this crazy?" she said putting her arms around Alex and laying her head on her shoulder.

"No, it's not crazy. I don't think we've been apart since after the wedding," Alex said pulling Riley close.

"We haven't. How am I going to get to sleep tonight without you holding me?"

"You'll have to use your imagination and feel my arms around you like they were last night."

"I have a better idea," Riley said, pushing Alex up against the wall and kissing her possessively.

"What are you doing?" Alex said a little out of breath.

"I'm giving you something to remember until I get back home next week." With that Riley crushed her lips to Alex's and slid her hands under her shirt. She caressed Alex's breasts and pinched her nipples, feeling them harden through her bra. Alex's breath caught in her throat when Riley began nipping and kissing her neck, and then she was in her ear. "You are so sexy I can't keep my hands off you."

Riley's hand slid down under Alex's waistband and into her panties. "Oh, baby, you are so wet. Do you know what that does to me?" Alex slapped her hands against the wall to hold herself up.

Riley pushed her fingers down Alex's slit to her opening and back up, finding her bud was hot to the touch. "Oh my god," Alex panted. Riley continued this pattern and then teased Alex's opening before thrusting two fingers inside. Alex's knees went weak, and she would have slid down the wall if Riley wasn't holding her up. Riley continued in and out, deeper and deeper, as she nipped and kissed Alex's neck. When she could tell Alex was close, Riley whispered, "Let go, baby, I've got you."

Alex moaned, and Riley swallowed her cry with a kiss as Alex came undone. Riley kept her fingers inside as Alex rode the waves of her orgasm. When her breathing started to slow, Riley whispered, "You won't forget that, will you?"

"Good god, no," Alex said putting her arms around Riley in a bear hug, picking her up and dropping her on the bed. She was on Riley in an instant pulling her shorts and panties down. "You don't get to have all the fun." She spread Riley's legs wide and came up to kiss her while her hand found what she wanted. Riley was soaking wet.

"I think you liked that almost as much as I did," Alex growled. She kissed Riley again, taking her breath away as her fingers found her bud. Alex looked into Riley's eyes as her breath came faster and faster. With a hint of a smile she placed both hands under Riley's thighs, bending her knees, then she dove in for a taste. Riley writhed beneath her, fisting her hands into the bedspread. Alex made love with her tongue, in and out, licking and sucking until Riley let out a cry as her legs tensed and her hands came to Alex's head, holding her in place. The orgasm began to soften, and Riley straightened her legs and threw her arms on the bed, gulping for breath. Alex plopped down beside her.

"My god!" Riley said.

"You can say that again!"

Riley turned just her head and looked at Alex. Alex turned her head, and when their eyes met, they started giggling. Riley turned on her side, and Alex rolled onto hers and said, "That's the best sex I've ever had with my clothes on."

"That's the best sex I've ever had with half my clothes on," replied Riley.

Their giggles burst into full-blown laughter. Riley cupped the side of Alex's face. "I'm going to miss you so much."

Alex leaned in and kissed her. "Then hurry home."

13

The day after Alex left Riley was busy putting the last load of clothes in her car to take to the women's shelter when Keith and Jenn drove up along with Kevin and Jodie. She watched them get out of the car and immediately felt that something was off.

"Hey, what are y'all doing here," she said cheerily. "I'm sure I could find something for you to do."

Keith stopped in front of her and said, "We need to talk to you before you make a horrible mistake."

Riley narrowed her eyes at him, "A horrible mistake?" She looked to Jenn and Jodie and could see how uncomfortable they were.

"Can we go inside and talk?" Kevin said.

"Sure," Riley said leading the way. She knew exactly what was about to happen. She could feel it. This was about Alex. She was ready.

Once inside Keith said, "You may want to sit down."

"I'm fine," Riley said standing while everyone else found a seat.

"Look Riley, how much do you know about Alex," Keith began.

"I know more than you do and you can stop right there."

"Then you know that she's a sex offender," said Kevin.

"I do and I'm pretty sure you don't know why she's considered a sex offender, do you?"

"It doesn't matter," said Keith.

"It does matter, Keith. What is this, did you plan to wait until Alex left to gang up on me and tell me about my girlfriend's past?"

"It's not like that Riley," said Jodie.

"Do you have any idea what this will do to your life and your reputation?" said Kevin.

"My reputation? When did you give a shit about my reputation and the key word is MY."

The front door opened and Rachel and Amy walked in. They walked over one on either side of Riley and Amy said, "What do you think you're doing to Aunt Riley?"

"This is none of your business, Amy," said Kevin. "You and Rachel go home."

"I think it is our business, Uncle Kevin," said Rachel. "We overheard you planning to surprise Aunt Riley with dirt on Alex. Who does that to their own sister?"

"We're trying to keep her from ruining her life," said Keith.

"Ruining my life? Do you hear yourselves? I'm a grown woman."

"Riley, I don't really want to say anything in front of the girls," said Kevin quietly.

"Let me take care of that for all of you," Riley said. She then retold Alex's story, including the crime, punishment, why she left Texas and stayed in St. John. Riley left nothing out and even told them about the few times she'd been treated poorly in St. John. The silence was deafening when she finished speaking.

Riley looked around the room at her family and said with tears in her eyes, "I will not stand here and let you say anything against Alex or me. We will hear plenty of that in the future and my family will not be those people."

There was a knock on the door and Kara walked in with Sara and Julie. She went to Riley and put her arm around her shoulder.

"I don't know which one of you made her cry, but I'm telling you to leave her alone!" Kara said her voice rising. "Riley James is the best person I know. She knows exactly who Alex Adams is. She is the person that was made for Riley and she finally found her. And no one is going to try and stop them from living their love. Do you hear me? No one!"

Riley looked at Kara blinking back tears.

"We stand with Riley," said Sara. "And I'll say this. I found out about Alex not long after I left St. John. The Alex I knew and the Alex that made Riley so happy couldn't be the same person that was on that registry. I knew there was more to the story. And I trusted Alex to tell her story to Riley and she did."

Riley smiled at Sara and said, "Thanks for giving her that chance." Sara nodded.

Kara faced Riley and said, "You don't have to answer any more questions about Alex, not with us. We're your friends, we love you, we trust you and we love Alex too."

Amy and Rachel put their arms around Riley from behind and said, "We do too."

Jenn stood up and looked from Keith to Kevin, "I told you this was a bad idea." And then to Riley she said, "I tried to tell them to trust you but, your idiotic big brothers don't listen sometimes."

"I may be an idiot, but I love my little sister and don't want people harassing her," explained Keith.

"Aren't you doing the exact same thing?" said Jodie.

Keith and Kevin looked at one another and stood up. "I'm not sorry that I care about my sister," said Kevin walking to the door. "But this isn't getting us anywhere." He and Kevin walked out.

"Go tell your dad we're riding with you," Jenn said to Rachel.

Riley looked at the women gathered in her living room, took a deep breath and said with a weak smile, "Give me just a sec." She walked out of the room into her bedroom. Thoughts of Alex ran through her head as she sat down on the bed. She knew there was going to be some kind of confrontation with her brothers, but never dreamed it would be like this. They always trusted her judgement and talked with her, not to her like they did today. After gathering herself she walked back into the living room.

She looked at Kara, "Question, how did you know something was going on?"

"Well, Alex texted me yesterday and said she had a bad feeling around Keith. She didn't get the opportunity to talk to him before she left so she asked me to watch out for you. I reached out to Rachel and Amy. When they overheard their parents last night they called me."

Riley nodded.

Jenn spoke up and said, "I'm sorry we blindsided you like that. I should have warned you."

"Surely you two don't agree with them," Riley said looking from Jenn to Jodie.

"I will admit, when Kevin told me about it, I was scared

for you. But this was not the way to handle it and Jenn and I tried to make them see that and let us talk to you first."

Riley didn't know what to say, this was a lot to take in. On one hand it was nice having her family and friends rally around her but then, there were her brothers that thought she was ruining her life. If they only knew, Alex had given her a *life*. Sure, they can see how happy she is now, but they didn't know how lonely she was before. They didn't know she'd almost given up finding someone to share her life.

"Hey, it's going to be alright," Kara said bringing her back to the group.

"I know it is. And I know from time to time Alex's past is going to come up. What I didn't expect was my brothers' reaction." Riley looked around the room and let out a deep breath, "But that's okay. I've got a house to pack up and a life to live."

"You sure do. Put us to work," said Amy.

"Thank you all for your support. I can't tell you how much it means to me."

"Alex is one lucky woman," said Julie.

"So am I."

* * *

Alex made it back home with no problems. She couldn't believe how much she missed Riley. Her bad feeling about Keith was warranted when Riley recounted what happened. It hurt Alex that Riley had to go through that because of her. She knew this wouldn't be the only time something like this happened but, this was Riley's family. Alex never wanted to come between her and her family but, Riley reassured her everything would be alright.

The house seemed empty. Riley called her every day to

give her updates on the packing, storing, and when she'd be back. Alex tried to busy herself with chores around the house as well as at the bar. There was just so much she could clean. The house was spotless; she did maintenance and finished a few things she wanted to do to spruce up Peaches. Liz commented on how much she was working, but Alex explained that the house was too quiet. She might as well be working instead of sitting around missing Riley. Thank goodness she'd be back in two more days. *Two more long days,* Alex thought.

She tried to remember her life before Riley. It didn't compare to life after Riley when living had become so much more. She and Liz were sitting on the patio before Peaches opened for the evening when Alex said, "I'm going to ask Riley to marry me."

"Well, how about that. It's about time," Liz said.

"What do you mean, it's about time?"

"I'm surprised you waited so long."

"I thought with all the life-changing decisions she'd been making that it'd be best to let her settle in before making another one," Alex explained.

"Did you ever think that maybe it would make all those other decisions a lot easier for her?"

"Hmm, I never thought about that," Alex said.

"So when and how do you plan to do this?"

"I'm not sure. I don't really want to wait any longer, and I'm not sure where. I thought maybe that special place of ours at the park would be good. I've got to come up with something to make it spectacular like she is. Any ideas?"

"Have you got a ring? You might want to start with that."

"I've thought about that. Is that something we should choose together, or do I get it and hope she likes it?"

"I'm pretty sure you know her well enough by now that whatever you choose she'll love."

"She will say yes, right?"

Liz laughed. "I can't think of one reason she wouldn't."

"This has been the longest week of my life, and these last two days seem to be dragging even more."

"Do you have any idea how happy I am for you? You are a different person. You're happy all the time, you're doing more than merely working or working out. And Riley... now that is one special woman."

"Don't I know it! How in the world did I get so lucky?"

"I'm not sure it has anything to do with luck. Yes, she has been good for you and given you a life, but you've done a lot for her, too. I think she had resigned herself to being alone just as you had. It was meant to be and at the right time."

Alex sat there smiling and nodding in agreement.

Liz had a few plans to make herself. Little did Alex know but Riley would be back tomorrow. She had called Liz and asked her to help get Alex to their place at the park the following evening not long before sunset. Riley had a surprise for Alex that she hoped she'd never forget.

* * *

Riley and Kara put the last of Riley's things into storage and were sitting on Kara's patio having a well-deserved beer. Riley was closing on the house tomorrow. She had gotten rid of everything that the buyers weren't keeping, so she was spending this last night with Kara.

What a week! They had worked all day every day, so Riley could get back to St. John a day early. She planned to surprise Alex at their special place with Liz's help.

"So Liz has a way to get Alex to the park for your surprise?" Kara asked.

"She said she would take care of it. Mandy is meeting me at the airport, then taking me there to help set everything up. We're going to hang lights from the trees over a blanket on the ground. I'm going to get food and have a bottle of champagne ready. I have a speaker that I'm planning to play some of our favorite songs through to set the mood."

"This sounds really nice, Riley. It'll knock her socks off, if she was wearing any, which we know she won't be."

They laughed. "She's the one, Kara," Riley said. "I've never been so sure of anything in my life. She is my life! This is what Kim and Kerry talk about. Sure, I've been in love before, but this is even more. One night, before you came back, while we were still on 'vacation,' we sat down at the end of the beach near our hotel. Alex had brought a few things to snack on, and we talked. There wasn't anyone around, and the sun had set. There was a comfortable silence between us, and we sat there holding hands. I remember thinking, *this* must be what heaven is like. We looked into one another's eyes and we kissed."

"Well, don't stop there!"

Riley chuckled. "That kiss! I had never felt anything like it. It's like our hearts became one. Mine went down into her chest, and hers came into mine. It's hard to explain, but that's when I knew." She sighed and continued. "It scared me. I felt so vulnerable, you don't know if the other person feels the same way. I wanted to say something but couldn't."

"What did Alex do?"

"We kept staring into one another's eyes. I hoped she was feeling the same thing. Now I know we were both afraid to say anything. I'm nearly fifty years old, and I was afraid of what another person would say! I guess it doesn't matter how old you are, when you're putting your heart out there, you want the other person to feel the same but, it takes courage to do it."

"And aren't you glad you found that courage?"

"Am I ever! And I've got to find that courage again tomorrow evening when we're both at the park and I propose. You can't believe how nervous I am."

"I'm sure you are, but you know she's going to say yes."

"I don't know it, but I sure hope so."

"She will. Alex is as crazy about you as you are about her."

Riley chuckled. "I am crazy about her, you've got that right."

"I expect a full recap tomorrow night. I want all the details," said Kara.

"Well if it goes like I'm hoping, you'll have to wait until the next day."

"Understood. Wishing you luck, that you don't need," Kara said reaching her bottle out to Riley's. They clinked bottles and smiled.

* * *

Everything was coming together. Riley's plane was late, but Mandy got her to the park, and they had the lights up, music ready to play, and champagne chilling. Riley looked around and surveyed the scene. "Okay. Everything looks ready."

"Have you heard from Liz?" Mandy asked.

"She texted just now and said Alex is on the way. She's hiding at the park entrance and will text when Alex passes through. From there it should be less than five minutes before she sees the sign and starts down the trail. You're sure she'll be able to hear the music?"

"I'm sure. I could hear it when you had me walk down the trail. Calm down."

"Calm down? That's easy for you to say, Mandy. This is the most important moment of my life!"

Mandy smiled and walked over to Riley. She took her by the shoulders and said, "Close your eyes."

"What?"

"Just listen to me for a minute. Close your eyes." Riley did as Mandy told her.

"Now take a deep breath, slowly in and slowly out."

Riley took a deep breath as Mandy instructed.

"Good, do it again."

Riley continued until she'd taken five deep breaths.

"Now, open your eyes. Better?" Mandy asked.

"Yes, my heart isn't about to explode. It's just pounding," Riley said, chuckling.

Riley's phone pinged. She looked down at it and took a deep breath. "That's Liz," she said, reading the text. "She made it through the gate."

"Okay. That's my cue to leave." Mandy hugged Riley. "You've got this." Then she ran down to the water and left along the beach until she disappeared into some nearby trees.

Riley looked around the clearing one more time. She was nervous, but somehow knowing Alex was near calmed her. All she wanted to do was run to Alex and hug her, but she would control herself because she wanted to tell Alex just how much she meant to her. She had thought about what she wanted to say but instead of memorizing a speech she'd likely forget, she decided she'd wait for the right words at that moment. She started the music and waited.

Alex couldn't figure out what was going on. Liz had called and said her Jeep was stuck in the park and asked if Alex would come help her. When she came through the park and went to where Liz was supposed to be, she couldn't see the Jeep anywhere. Then something caught her eye. She kept going, and in the distance, she could see a sign right at the trail to her and Riley's place. As she got closer, she pulled over. The sign was simply an arrow pointing down the trail. That was strange.

She got out of her SUV and started walking down the trail. After a few steps she heard something. She stopped and listened; it was music. After a few more steps she realized that it was one of her and Riley's favorite songs. Alex started walking faster. Surely it couldn't be, Riley wasn't supposed to be back until tomorrow.

When she broke through the trees, there was Riley across the clearing, standing near a blanket with twinkling lights in the trees above her. She had on the dress that she wore the night of Kim and Kerry's wedding, the one that took Alex's breath away, the one she couldn't wait to take off her. Alex hesitated for a moment to take it all in. This was like a dream. Riley was so beautiful, waiting on her, and then she smiled. Alex thought her heart would explode with love. She started walking forward as if Riley was pulling her over with just her eyes.

When she got close, Riley held out her hands. Alex took them both in hers, the biggest smile lighting up her entire face. "What is all this?" Alex asked.

"I had something important I needed to ask you, and this is the best place to do that."

"Okay," Alex said a question in her voice.

Riley reached up and kissed Alex on the cheek and then lowered herself to one knee. Alex's eyes couldn't get any bigger! Riley's heart was thumping, but she felt a certain calm looking up into them.

"When I was a kid, I would imagine that someday a beautiful woman was going to sweep me away to live happily ever after," Riley began. "As time went along, I still believed that beautiful woman would find me eventually. And Alex, you finally did. You found me and swept me into your world, and it's better than any I could've ever imagined. You have given me and shown me love that can only be felt and lived in. There are no words to describe what you do to my heart, mind, and body, my life. I love you so very much. Alex Adams, will you marry me?"

Alex lowered to her knees in front of Riley and took her face in her hands. With tears in her eyes she said, "Yes." She placed her lips on Riley's in such a tender kiss. She pulled away, still holding Riley's face, and said, "Riley, you saved me. I had a glimmer of hope that someday I would find that special someone meant for me, but I thought I was being foolish. When I first saw you and our eyes met, something shifted inside me and I knew I'd never be the same. I was afraid to believe it was real, but my heart wouldn't let me ignore it. Thank goodness we found one another." With that their lips met, and the kiss went on and on.

When they finally pulled back, Riley threw her head back and yelled, "Woohoo! She said yes!" She threw her arms around Alex, and they tumbled over on the blanket both laughing.

"You know when you wear that dress, I'm going to take it right back off," Alex stated as she rolled on top of Riley.

"That's what I was counting on," Riley said with her best seductive smile.

Alex ran her hand over Riley's hip and a daring eyebrow popped up. "And you're not wearing anything under it!"

Riley smiled a little shyly now. "I was hopeful."

Alex laughed, then stilled, hovering over Riley. "I missed you and now I'm going to show my fiancée just how much."

Later, during a night swim, with the moon shining down on them, Riley made Alex hers. As they lay on the blanket letting their bodies dry, Alex rolled onto her elbow. She didn't mind that Riley had proposed first, maybe they could get married sooner. "How long are you going to make me wait to marry you?"

"You don't want to be engaged for a while?"

"I do not. Don't you think we waited long enough to find one another? I don't want to lose another minute," Alex said.

"I agree, but..."

"But?" Alex said raising an eyebrow.

"But there are people that want to be here when we do this. What would you think about getting married in June?"

"I think that's nine months away! That's too long!"

"Wait, hear me out," Riley said, rolling onto her elbow and running the back of her finger down Alex's cheek. "There's nothing I want to do more than marry you. I'd do it tomorrow, but I thought it would be appropriate if we get married on June fourth. That's one year after the day we met."

"Appropriate? I think tomorrow would be more appropriate."

Riley gazed into Alex's eyes, deep in thought. She looked at that most beautiful face, saw the love in those eyes that was only meant for her, and she couldn't ask her to wait. "I don't know what to do. I wanted Liz to marry us, and I thought all our family and friends could be here if we did it in June. But the way you're looking at me, I don't want to wait either."

Alex took a strand of Riley's hair and curled it around her ear. They both kept gazing and thinking until Alex said, "I like the idea of June fourth and Liz marrying us. I don't know how I'll ever wait that long, though."

"I have an idea. I've thought about starting a bucket list," explained Riley.

"A bucket list? Like places you want to go or things you want to do before you die?"

"Sort of, but my bucket list is a little different."

"So?"

"My bucket list would be all the places I want to make love to you on the islands," said Riley.

Alex looked at her and smiled. "Where to first?"

14

Nine Months Later

"In about twenty-four hours you will be my wife," Riley said, sitting down in Alex's lap and putting her arms around her. They were taking a few moments to themselves before meeting their families and friends for the rehearsal dinner. There was a cool breeze caressing their bodies on the rooftop deck, and the sun was just beginning to change colors and bathe the horizon with the promise of a coming light show.

"I'm so relieved you and your brothers are on good terms. It only took nine months but, I was anxious about doing this without them."

"I know, I was too. But, it's our life Alex. And we're prepared to face anything together, they needed to understand that."

"I can't believe you made me wait this long, and I can't

believe I made it," Alex said kissing Riley softly. "There is something I need to talk to you about before we go to dinner, though."

"You sound awfully serious for someone that's about to make me the happiest woman alive," Riley said.

"One thing we never finalized was our last names," said Alex.

"Hmm, I guess we didn't. I figured we would hyphenate them, Adams-James or James-Adams. Which do you like?"

"I've thought about this quite a bit, and I'd like for us to go by James."

"Really? Why is that?"

"My past has messed up the name Alex Adams for me. It was okay in my childhood and before my mistake. I didn't realize it at the time, but the last sixteen years I've been waiting. Waiting for you, Riley, and here you are! Here we are! There is an 'us' now, and I can't tell you how good that feels. It's all because of you, so I want to be Alex James."

"So, you're telling me that when Liz declares us wife and wife tomorrow and we turn to the group, you want her to say, 'Let me present Riley and Alex James'?"

"Yes, exactly. The best part of my life began with you, Riley James, and that's why I want to be Alex James."

"I don't really know what to say, babe. This has taken me by surprise, but you have obviously put a lot of thought into it."

"I have," Alex said smiling. "So? Is it alright with you? Alex James?"

Riley looked at Alex with love spilling from her eyes. "I love you, Alex James." Then she kissed her tenderly, long and slow. Riley pulled back with a sigh. "Now I don't want to go to dinner."

"I know. We seem to keep doing this, don't we?" Alex said with a chuckle.

"We do, and I hope we never stop."

* * *

"I don't know how you got Alex to wait this long to get married," said Samantha. She and Rosie were standing with Kara and Riley as they watched people gather for the wedding on the beach.

"Oh, I found a few ways to keep her busy," Riley said, sneaking a look at Kara. They both laughed.

"Do I want to know?" Samantha said, looking from one to the other.

"What you don't know is that it was just as hard for me to wait as it was for her. We even played with the idea of getting married and just not telling anyone."

"Have you seen her today?" Rosie asked.

"Oh yeah, there's no way we were doing the 'not seeing the bride before the ceremony' thing," said Riley. "Our wedding is not full of tradition anyway. You have to admit the whole thing has been a bit out of the ordinary."

They all laughed. Riley started looking around a little nervously as it was almost time to start. "Where is my fiancée? She had better not be messing with me!"

"She wouldn't miss this for anything. She'll be here, Riley," Sam said, giving her a hug. "We'd better go take our seats. Come on, Rosie."

"I'll see you after you're a Missus." said Kara, hugging her close. "You're going to be a Missus! I'm so happy for you!"

Riley couldn't stop smiling thinking about that. She never thought it would happen. Being a Mrs. wasn't that big of a deal, she thought, but after they were engaged the idea of being Alex's wife meant so much to her.

Peaches was closed since they were having the wedding on the beach outside the patio. When Riley last saw Alex, she was making sure everything was ready for the party after. They were supposed to meet on the patio to walk down the aisle together, but she couldn't see Alex anywhere. Everyone else was there, and some were beginning to take their seats. Riley was beginning to get concerned when Max came out of the bar onto the patio and motioned her over.

"You're needed inside," he said, holding the door open for her.

She walked inside, and when the door closed, it was like entering another world. The bar was never this quiet. She looked around, and then she finally saw her. Alex was standing across from her in the corner of the dance floor. Her heart began beating out of her chest at the thought that this beautiful woman was about to become her wife. A smile broadened across Alex's face as she held out her hand. Riley walked over to her, and when she placed her hand in Alex's, she said, "May I have this dance?"

Riley smirked. "You do know there are several people outside waiting to see us get married."

"I do know that, but I wanted just a couple of minutes to hold you close, calm our hearts, and sway to the music before all the chaos started. You do kind of owe me for making me wait so long to marry you."

"Oh, all those bucket list payments weren't enough?" Riley asked, stepping into Alex's arms.

"Riley James, I will never get enough of you," Alex said, tenderly pulling her close.

ABOUT THE AUTHOR

Small town Texas girl that grew up believing she could do anything. Her mother loved to read and romance novels were a favorite that she passed on to her daughter. When she found lesfic novels her world changed. She not only fell in love with the genre, but wanted to write her own stories. You can find her books on Amazon and her website at jameymoodyauthor.com.

You can email her at jameymoodyauthor@gmail.com

A review would be appreciated and helps independent authors.

ALSO BY JAMEY MOODY

The Your Way Series:

Finding Home

Finding Family

Finding Forever

It Takes A Miracle

One Little Yes

The Lovers Landing Series

Where Secrets Are Safe

No More Secrets

And The Truth Is ...

Printed in Great Britain
by Amazon